The Treasure of the Long Sault

MONICA HUGHES

The Treasure of the Long Sault

A PANDA BOOK

General
PAPERBACKS

Toronto, Canada

A Panda Book published in 1990 by
General Paperbacks

Published by arrangement with
J.M. LeBel Enterprises Ltd.

Printed in the United States

The following dedication is adapted from the plaque erected by the Ontario-St. Lawrence Development Commission at Lake St. Lawrence, upon the lake's creation in July 1963:

In commemoration of the Battle of Crysler's Farm, this book is dedicated to the Canadian and American Nations whose common memories of old unhappy far-off things and battles long ago not only contribute to their separate heritages and traditions but form a bond between two friendly peoples.

The events of 1813 and the battle of Crysler's Farm are as true as recorded history can be, but Alexander MacAlpine and Bruce McIntosh are entirely imaginary characters and their adventures during the battle are fictitious. Similarly the descriptions of the work on the Seaway and Power Project, Upper Canada Village and the location of the new towns are factual, but Weaver's Landing and its inhabitants are imaginary, as, alas, is the treasure, although a dig was carried out at that time under the auspices of the Royal Ontario Museum.

The Treasure of the Long Sault

CHAPTER ONE

"Ten whole days holiday. I thought Easter would never come." Jamie Anderson bounced on the train seat and looked eagerly out of the window at the St. Lawrence River, full with spring run-off, a silver band cutting across the darkening evening.

"It's cool, all right." Neil hesitated. "But somehow, Jamie, I dread having to go back to Weaver's Landing again. I just wish Mother and Dad had found somewhere else to stay while the Project was on."

"None of the other people wanted to put us up. You know that, Neil."

"If only we could have stayed in Cornwall with the other Project staff . . . instead of out at MacAlpine's."

"Dad wanted to be close to the new town-sites. After all, that's where most of the work is. What on earth is wrong with it, anyway? Mrs. MacAlpine's great. She even bakes better than Mom, and she never tells me I've had enough when I haven't."

"Oh, sure, if you're talking about *food*. It's the place that's creepy. Every time we go back it's the same. You can feel them looking at you through those horrid little lace curtains when you go down the street. And one time when I went to the store for Mrs. MacAlpine there was a whole bunch of people in there, gossiping away. When I went in they all shut up. They didn't say one word the whole time I was in the store. They just stood there, looking at me. Sort of as if they hated me, but enjoyed hating me, too. And when I went out with the groceries I heard one of the women whisper to the others, 'Up at MacAlpine's.' The whole atmosphere down there, it's downright hostile."

"Whatever that means. Are you sure you not imagining the whole thing, Neil?"

"Of course not. I wouldn't imagine anything so spooky. Look, Jamie, haven't you noticed that none of the neighbours talk to Mrs. MacAlpine? Not even the mailman and he's a terrible gossip. I've got a horrible feeling that it's because of us."

"That's daft, Neil. Why should they hate us? They don't even know us. And we haven't done anything."

"We're Project people," Neil spoke gloomily.

"Some of them hate the Seaway and Power Project, so I guess they hate us too. I expect it's the same in town, too, but with so many people you wouldn't notice it. But in a village like Weaver's Landing . . . "

"That's the stupidest thing I ever heard of. They'll have the Seaway instead of that pokey little canal that's almost useless. And a wonderful new highway — Dad says Number Two Highway is nothing but a deathtrap. And a new town instead of this tacky little village. And the lake and the parkway."

Jamie's freckled face was red with indignation, and Neil burst out laughing. "Whoa. You don't have to convince me. But you've got to see it from their point of view. Lots of times people hate change, even if it's change for the better. They didn't ask to be moved. Hydro did it. And we're Hydro. And they hate us for it." He shivered. "I'm glad it's only ten days. I don't know how Mother can stand living down here the whole year."

"I think it's all in your mind. I'm glad I don't have an imagination. It's just a nuisance, especially when I'm going to be an engineer like Dad."

Neil grinned at his brother. Jamie was squarish and stocky, with curly red hair that glinted gold in the last traces of sun glancing in through the passing trees. He had a whole Milky Way of freckles across his nose and cheekbones, and his bold blue eyes twinkled. He looked like Dad, a hundred percent practical Scots.

Neil sighed. It must be great to be so sure of oneself. Jamie was twelve years old and he knew exactly what he wanted out of life, and Neil could bet he would get it too. As for himself, he was almost fourteen and he hadn't a clue. He looked absently at his reflection in the train window, the pale triangular shaped face, the image of his mother's, the dark red hair falling over his hazel eyes. He brushed it impatiently out of the way and looked over at his brother.

"Just coming into Iroquois. Won't be long now. Just imagine it two years from now, Jamie. There'll be water swirling in the doors and windows of those houses over there. Over the rosebushes."

"That's daft, Neil. You know Dad told us that the houses that aren't worth moving will be torn down and the whole area smoothed over for beaches."

"Yeah, I know. But it's more interesting thinking of a flooded town if you imagine the houses and gardens are still there. Don't you ever think of things like that, Jamie?"

"Nope. It'd be a waste of time. I think of how many cubic yards of glacial till are going into the dykes and how many kilowatts of electricity the dam will produce. That *is* exciting."

Neil shook his head and looked out of the window as the train pulled out of the station. Sometimes he felt mixed up, as if he were two people inside, his practical Scots father, his imaginative Huguenot-New England mother. It would be neat to be like Dad. But an engineer . . . ?

"Morrisburg! Next stop Morrisburg!"

The boys grabbed their bags and walked down the aisle to the door. "Too bad this train doesn't stop at Weaver's Landing. We'll have quite a walk."

"Oh, we're sure to be able to hitch a ride with all the holiday traffic bound for Montreal. And that milk train we usually catch is gruesome. Jolly lucky old Higgins let us off early. A whole extra night at home. We'll really surprise Mom and Dad."

They walked south to the river and turned left along the highway. There was indeed plenty of traffic and they hadn't been walking for more than five minutes before a car pulled out of the traffic and a voice called to them.

"Looking for a ride? Going far?"

"Just the next village. Thank you, sir."

They scrambled in and their driver eased back into the traffic. The narrow tree-lined road twisted and turned, hugging the contours of the river, which fell away to their right, marred by the scruffy little weekend cottages that clung to the steep banks.

"This highway's a disgrace," their driver grunted. "I'll be glad when the new highway's operational. Where do you boys want off?"

"Just around the next bend, sir. The last house on the left. The one with the big white porch."

The driver slowed to twenty and slid through the village, past the dozen houses, the litte grocery store, the gas station.

"No house with a white porch. Sure you have the right place, boys? These villages all look alike to me."

"I'm sure, sir. Our parents have been staying here for nearly two years. We *couldn't* have made a mistake." Neil spoke out firmly, but into his mind flashed a spooky story he'd read, about a girl at the Paris Exposition who returned to her hotel after an hour's absence to find no brother, no luggage, no room, and all the staff denying that they'd ever stayed there. He shivered. Supposing . . . ?

Jamie started laughing "Look, Neil, over there. That's the MacAlpine house." He pointed at a deep square hole beside the road, surrounded by stones standing a foot above the ground like a castle battlement.

"What on earth?" exclaimed their driver.

"They've moved the house, Neil."

"Of course! But I can't think why they didn't tell us."

"Suppose they thought they'd surprise us when we came in on the milk train tomorrow."

"They surprised us all right." Neil said ruefully. He still felt shaky inside.

"Moved the house?" The driver leaned out of his window. "A big house, you said, with a *porch*?"

"Yes," Jamie said proudly. "Five bedrooms and a porch and a summer kitchen. It's an old house, built around 1800. Dad's the engineer in charge of moving the houses and things before the flooding."

The driver whistled. "Some job. How many houses?"

"About five hundred. And about forty miles of railway and highway."

"Amazing. But what about you boys? You want to go into one of the neighbours' here?"

"No!" Neil's voice was sharp and he saw the driver look at him curiously. He made his voice casual. "No, thanks. It's all right. Could you drop us off at Farran Point? It's about five miles up the highway. We can walk into the new town from there."

"Okay, then." The driver eased the car back into the traffic. "But if you don't know where your house is how are you going to find it?"

"Oh, they must have just started moving the houses up there. We'll just have to look around."

"Fair enough. Sorry I can't take you right up there, but I'm running late as it is." He negotiated the twisting narrow road with care. "Is this Farran Point coming up now? Good. You boys'll need a flashlight. It's as dark as pitch tonight."

"Got your flashlight, Jamie?"

"Of course I have. I always have my flashlight."

"That's all right then. Good luck, boys."

"Thank you, sir. Goodnight."

Neil and Jamie walked due north up the wide road to the new townsite. The moonless sky pulsed with stars and ahead of them was a flickering green arch of Northern Lights.

"This is fun, Jamie. Aren't the stars super."

"If I wasn't going to be an engineer I guess I'd be an astronaut." Jamie shifted his bag to his other hand.

"Need help with that?"

"Course I don't. What do you take me for?" He punched his brother lightly in the ribs. They scuffled for a minute and then walked on up the road. The packed gravel changed to cement. They had arrived. Neil stopped and looked round curiously. It was a strange feeling, like being in some sort of ghost town. The new pavement and sidewalks curved around, gleaming in the flashlight beam. The street lights shone like sparks in the blackness. The lots stood empty. It was very quiet. As their eyes grew accustomed they could see, here and there, lonely as islands in a vast sea, houses that had already been moved, perhaps half a dozen in the whole town.

"There it is, Jamie, over there." Neil tried to speak casually. His imagination had been working overtime as they had walked up the access road to the townsite. Suppose their houses *hadn't* been there.

"Good, I'm hungry. Hope Mrs. MacAlpine's got something on."

"It's awfully late, Jamie. I never thought. We should have stopped to eat in Morrisburg. Mrs. MacAlpine's not expecting us till lunchtime tomorrow, remember."

"She'll have something." Jamie's life was always comfortably sure. He ran up the porch steps and banged on the door. It opened and brightness and warmth poured out into the night.

"Neil, Jamie! What a surprise. Come away in!"

It was warm and bright in the little hall with the shining brass pots and the old mahogany clock ticking in its accustomed corner. The boys looked around appreciatively.

"It's just the way it always was. When did they move you?"

"The day before yesterday. I didna even take the dishes out of the cupboards. and not a dish broken nor a crack in the plaster. I wish you had been here to see it."

"Dad should have waited. He knew I wanted to watch. Where are they, Mrs. MacAlpine?"

"Och, they went off to a movie in Cornwall, seeing as they weren't expecting you till the morn. And foreby, what are you doing here?"

"They let us out of school early. We just made the fast train. Got a lift from Morrisburg. You should have seen Neil's face when we got to Weaver's Landing!"

"Did you get your dinner on the train then? No? You must be fair clemmed with hunger then. Isn't it a piece of luck that I've the remains of the stew from supper. I'll just pop it back on the stove and we'll have you fed in a flash."

Twenty minutes later Neil sopped up the last of the gravy with a chunk of home-made bread. He leaned back in his chair and sighed. "Oh, that was splendid, Mrs. MacAlpine. I can't tell you what the food at school is like."

"Och, away with you. You both look healthy enough to me. And you've grown since Christmas."

"I expect that's all the running around the playing fields before breakfast. Before *breakfast*, Mrs. MacAlpine!"

"Oh, never Jamie! Have you had enough, now, or could you fancy a wee piece of cake?"

"Yes, please."

"Neil?"

"No, thank you. I couldn't manage another thing." Neil got up and looked past the crisp kitchen curtains at the blackness outside. "It's really weird, not seeing the river from this window any more. Does it bother you, Mrs. MacAlpine?"

"It does not. I'm right glad to have moved and that's the truth of it." She cleared the dishes off the table with an emphatic nod and began to run the water in the sink.

"I'll do the dishes. You sit in the rocker and talk to us. You must be tired."

"Thank you, Neil. I am that. The last two days have been a bit of a turmoil."

Neil swished the suds around in the sink. "What did you mean, you were so glad to have moved?"

Mrs. MacAlpine leant back in the rocker, took up her knitting from the basket by the stove and sighed. "Och, it's hard to put into words. The neighbours. The whispering and the backbiting. If I'd known the truth of it when I married MacAlpine I'd have made him sell the store and take me away. But not one word did he tell me of the story, not till I forced him to. Maybe he didn't know how bad it would be. Maybe it was only the womenfolk that kept the whole scandal alive . . . " She sighed and knitted, rocking gently.

"Mrs. MacAlpine, do you mean the way people act at Weaver's Landing has nothing to do with us? That it's not our fault they're that way?"

"Your fault? Och, my poor wee lad. Of course not. I didn't know they were taking it out on you. Well, there's prejudice for you. It spreads like the measles."

"I don't understand. What is it? I was so sure it was us they were hating."

"I'd better tell you the whole story, Neil, and get it out in the open. Though the way the folk at Weaver's Landing gossip it's hardly the big secret." She sighed and looked at the carriage clock on the mantel above the stove. "Your parents won't be back for another hour. Set you down and I'll tell you the story that no one around here will ever let me forget, the story of my husband's grandfather, Alexander MacAlpine, and how he was a traitor to his country."

CHAPTER TWO

"It all happened way back in the war with the Americans," Mrs. MacAlpine began, settling back in the rocker by the stove and taking up her knitting.

"But we weren't at war with the Americans," Jamie protested. "We were always on the same side."

"Och, indeed we were. Back in 1812. And a great bit of foolishness it seems to have been. But was there ever a war that wasna?"

"1812!" Neil counted. "But that's about a hundred and fifty years ago. Your husband's grandfather couldn't possibly have been there."

"Indeed he was. He was twenty years old at the time of the battle, but he didn't marry for many years after. Truth to tell, it seems that none of the young girls in the Counties would have him, on account of the story of him being a traitor and all. But eventually he found a lass in Montreal and brought her home to Weaver's Landing. My Alec's father, Jock, was born in this very house in 1840. Jock had to find a bride outside the counties too, and Alec, my husband, was born here in 1871. Alec was a middle-aged man when he brought me to Weaver's Landing from Ottawa. I knew nothing of the story, you ken. Alec and I had forty years together." She sighed and Neil saw her twisting the broad gold band on her gnarled finger. "He was a fine man and a good provider. But not telling me the story of his grandfather Alexander has been mighty hard to forgive, even after all these years."

"Why didn't you make him take you away, Mrs. MacAlpine?"

"Och, Neil, I often wondered that myself. And why Jock didna leave, nor Alexander himself, come to that. But the MacAlpines settled on the St. Lawrence after the American War of Independence, and they had just started to make a good life for themselves. They were merchants and canny ones at that. To dig up your roots once and start again, this is fine. It can give you new courage, a new peek at life. But to have to go on doing it, that takes the heart out of a man."

"I see." Neil spoke thoughtfully. "I suppose it would

have seemed like an admission of guilt, too, if they had left?"

"Aye, that too."

"But guilt about what? You still haven't told us what happened." Jamie was always impatient to get to the meat of a thing.

"Och, well. I cannot tell you all the ins and outs of it, for I didna take much history at school. But I know that back in November of 1813 a big American force was going by road and river to try and capture Montreal, with British and Canadian soldiers coming up behind them. The British Commander stayed at John Crysler's farm overnight . . . "

"But we've seen that," Jamie interrupted excitedly. "That's one of the houses they're moving into the new park. It's real!"

"Of course it's real, you nut. Just because a thing happened a hundred and fifty years ago doesn't make it any less real. Do go on, Mrs. MacAlpine."

"Well, it seems that early in the morning someone gave the alarm to the American troops and they opened fire. As it happened they lost the battle and decided not to try and take Montreal that winter. Which was lucky for Alexander, for one of the Indian scouts from St. Regis found him hiding in a ravine way over among the American troops. They took him to Crysler's Farm for questioning. If we'd lost the battle I expect they'd have shot him there and then. But they had no proof that he'd given away the British positions to the Americans. They didna believe him but they let him go. But nobody ever let him forget, nor his son, nor his son's son. There's wars for you!" Her voice was bitter.

"But what *was* Alexander's story, Mrs. MacAlpine? What did he say he'd been doing that night?"

"Och, he had a story so crazy that nobody would believe it. Now if he'd said he'd been out courting a girl, though it would be pretty hard to swallow on a snowy wet November night, he just might have been believed. But no. He would have it that he'd been out with his friend Bruce McIntosh, hunting for treasure — Indian treasure, of all things. When they captured Alexander, Bruce wasna with him. And I guess he never came forward later, or Alexander might have been believed."

"And that's the whole story?"

"Aye, that's the sum total of it."

"It doesn't seem like very much, for the neighbours to go on being beastly to you all this time later."

"Och, I've just given you the bare bones of the truth as I know it. The way it's been fleshed out over the years, you would hardly credit. If you listen to the people around here, especially in Weaver's Landing,

Alexander MacAlpine was as great a traitor as Benedict Arnold."

"Can't you get them to believe the truth? It isn't fair, them being so mean to you."

"Och, Neil, don't get yourself all stirred up about it. My shoulders are broad." She sighed. "Though I'd dearly love to know the truth of it for my own peace of mind. As for the neighbours, since when was any kind of prejudice fair? And it's not something you can talk people out of. You've got to show them the truth, and then maybe the next time they'll have a mite more sense."

"I bet he wasn't a traitor. I bet he really was hunting secret treasure. Don't you think so, Neil? Neil!"

"What? Oh, I agree. I think Alexander's story is so wild it simply has to be true. If there was only some way we could prove it. Mrs. MacAlpine, *are* there any stories about Indian treasure? I didn't know Indians went in for collecting valuables that way, you know, like Spanish pirates or Vikings. But Indians?"

"Why, yes." Mrs. MacAlpine was puzzled. "There's always been some sort of story about a great Indian treasure hereabouts. But nobody gives any heed to it at all."

"Anyway, Neil, I don't see that it matters whether there really was a treasure or not. If Alexander thought there was, that's what counts.

"Good thinking, Jamie."

"Aren't there any other clues at all, Mrs. MacAlpine? Do think," Jamie begged.

"Not a single one." She was emphatic. "You can imagine how I have scoured this house a dozen times, and Jock's wife and maybe Alexander's too must have done the same thing, looking for some hint of the diary. But not a trace has ever been found."

"What diary?" the boys chorused.

"Alexander's diary, of course. Didna I tell you? Well, when he was dying Alexander tried to tell his wife where he'd hidden something. He said, 'The truth . . . where I wrote the truth . . . tell Jock.' But they never found it."

"It didn't have to be a diary. Just any old piece of paper."

"I suppose not. But it was known that he kept diaries, so I guess it was taken for granted."

"Anyway it's still a clue. We need more. If we could only think back to what Alexander was really doing that night. Mrs. MacAlpine, do you have a map — a survey-type map, not just a road one?"

"Aye. Just of the Counties, Neil. Wait on a moment." She bustled out of the kitchen. Neil cleared the coffee pot and the bowl of African violets off the kitchen table and spread out the map she brought him.

"Now let's see if I can remember the history we did last term. Look, Mrs. MacAlpine, Jamie. North of the St. Lawrence here the United Empire Loyalists have just settled and begun farming. There are little groups of houses, a kirk, maybe a schoolhouse. The King's Road is a broad dirt track running from Montreal, west to Kingston and York, parallel to the river. The river is still the easiest form of transportation, except in the rapids section. North of the river is nothing but wilderness.

"Over in Europe Napoleon is running wild. He's already run out of money and sold Louisiana to the Americans to get more funds for his war to conquer Europe. The British have just got him out of Spain, but in 1812 he turns his eyes towards Russia. England is constantly threatened with invasion and runs a blockade to cut off France's supplies. The Americans are angry at the blockade which interferes with their trade, but eventually an agreement is reached between the British and the Americans.

"Unfortunately, by the time a sailing boat gets back to America with the news, war has already started. The history books call it the War of Poor Communications."

"You mean if there'd been a hot line between Washington and London the war wouldn't have happened?"

Right. But back then the fastest thing was a sailing ship or a man on a horse. To the ordinary farmer with no radio or even newspaper the whole thing must have seemed an extraordinary muddle, anyway." Neil bent over the map and traced the blue strip of the river with his finger. "In October of 1813 the American Major General Wilkinson with an army of eight thousand men is starting down the St. Lawrence River from Sackets Harbor, bound on capturing Montreal. In fact, the American War Council has already decided to stop hostilities for the winter, but Wilkinson hasn't received word of this. So with three hundred small boats and about a dozen gunboats he sets off down river, with a small force of about six hundred British and Canadian soldiers in pursuit.

"Where the river narrows, here, at Prescott and Ogdensburg, the Americans come under fire from farmers and militiamen on the shore. In the boats they are exposed and helpless, so Wilkinson decides to land his force on the North shore and march down the King's Road to Montreal, with just a few men to bring the boats down.

"By the night of November 10th it is cold and sleeting. The American boats have reached the top of the Long Sault Rapids and Wilkinson decides to wait out the bad weather. The British Lt. Colonel Morrison is close behind him, now with about nine hundred troops. He sets up his headquarters in John Crysler's farmhouse. That would be about here, wouldn't it, Mrs. MacAlpine? About half a mile upstream from Weaver's Landing?"

"Aye, that's about right, Neil."

"Okay. Morrison is in a good position. He has the river, flowing fast, at his right, and a swamp about half a mile inland on his left with wilderness behind it. Ahead of him a ploughed field planted in winter wheat gives him a good view, while beyond it are two gullies and a ravine — that must be the one, right by Weaver's Landing. He has three companies of Canadian Voltiguers scouting ahead as far as the ravine, and Indian scouts in the woods. They wait out the night, while the sleet falls. Next morning, Thursday November 11th, at eight o'clock, a shot rings out and the Americans open fire."

Neil stopped and looked up from the map. "According to my history book an Indian scout fired on an American reconnaissance patrol. But I don't suppose anyone would know for sure. Alexander must be hiding right in the ravine, here, since he is found close to the American lines. What is he doing there, crouched in a muddy ravine on a freezing wet dawn in the middle of a battle?"

"Perhaps he was a spy, after all." Jamie was matter-of-fact.

"Oh, honestly, Jamie, we're trying to prove he didn't do it, remember?"

"It's not very scientific. You should look at both sides of a question, Dad always says."

"People have been looking at the *one* side for a hundred and fifty years. Do you *mind* if we look at the other?"

"Okay. Go ahead."

"Thanks, chum. Look, to make sense of what Alexander is doing we simply must assume that he doesn't know the Americans are there, not till he's in the middle of them, I mean."

"He'd have had to see the troops and gunboats on the river."

"What if he'd gone *downriver* somewhere the previous evening?"

"He'd have bumped into the vanguard of the American troops somewhere along the road."

"Not if he was *on* the river, he wouldn't. For instance, suppose he was on one of the islands near the rapids. Remember, the gunboats are moored upstream of the rapids, so they could well have been hidden by one of the big islands, Goose Neck, maybe. Now suppose Alexander is hunting for treasure on some island near the Long Sault Rapids and at first light he rows quietly back upstream to Weaver's Landing. You see he'd have to wait for light before daring to negotiate the fast water. He creeps up the ravine, ready to go home to bed and whammo, he finds himself in the middle of a battlefield, being accused of being a spy."

"You know, that really doesn't sound bad, Neil. Though it doesn't explain about Alexander's friend Bruce. How on earth could we prove it?"

"Prove it! Something that happened a hundred and fifty years ago? I was just imagining how it might have happened."

"Imagining! That's the trouble with you, Neil. All ideas and no action."

"You just pipe down, Jamie Anderson."

"Shush, boys. Neil, that was very interesting. I wouldna be surprised if that was just the way of it. There now, I think I hear Mr. Anderson's car. Will they ever be surprised to see you!"

CHAPTER THREE

"Och, you'll never find the diary. I've searched the house from top to toe, and Alec's mother before me and his grandmother too, for all I know. But you're welcome to try. You can go over the house from cellar to attic, if you've a mind. In a manner of speaking, that is." Mrs. MacAlpine laughed and began to ladle out huge bowls of steaming porridge.

"What do you mean — In a manner of speaking?" Jamie dug his spoon in.

"That was just my wee joke. You know fine that the cellar here is brand new, with the old house set atop of it like a lid on a box. The old cellar is just a great hole back at Weaver's Landing. You saw it yourself on your way here yesterday."

"If they haven't filled it in yet." Neil looked up in

alarm. "We'll have to hurry up and search the old cellar before they fill it in."

Jamie went on calmly spooning in porridge. "They'll move all the houses first, Neil. Then they'll level off and tidy up the site. How come you never remember the things Dad tells us?"

"Less of that, young Jamie. Haven't you finished yet? We've got work to do."

"Suppose there isn't a diary?" Jamie objected as they went upstairs to brush their teeth.

"We know there's some sort of paper, Alexander said so. It's more likely to be a diary than anything. It's finding it that's going to be the catch. After all this time. Look at the stuff we lose ourselves."

"Yeah, but it's all this moving around from house to house and from school to home that loses things. Alexander stayed put all his life. Anyway, speak for yourself. It wasn't me lost all those library books."

Neil punched him in the ribs, and they had a short skirmish with pillows.

"Oh, bother. The feathers are coming out. Mrs. Mac will kill us."

"She won't. But Mother will. Shove the feathers back in, Jamie and I'll borrow a needle and thread from Mother's box."

"Don't let her see."

"I'm not stupid."

When Neil got back with the needle and thread and started cobbling the split pillow together, Jamie stared at him.

"Neil, how come you're so keen to treasure-hunt today? Last night it was just a story in history to you."

"Ouch!" Neil sucked his finger. "Oh, I started thinking about how crumby it was for Mrs. MacAlpine. She's been awfully good to us. I'd like it if we could find out some way of helping her. Anyway it'll be something to do in the holidays."

"You're going to get blood all over the pillow if you keep pricking your finger like that."

"I might do better if you'd stop kibbitzing. Jamie, why don't you go and ask Mother if we could have Mrs. MacAlpine make lunch for us to take out. Then we won't have to hurry back."

"What's this? Are you guys going to abandon me for the holidays? You only just got here."

Neil looked up to see his mother standing in the bedroom doorway. "Oh, Mother! We'll be home for dinner. And all evening — it'll be too dark to do much then. But, well . . . it's just that we've got things to do. You don't really mind, do you?"

Mother laughed. "I was only teasing. Have fun. But if you should go down to Weaver's Landing please keep out of the way of the house-moving gang. Having a father on the Project doesn't rate special privileges, you know. Anyway, I'd hate to see a house drop on you."

"We'll watch it. Honest. Mom, what are you hiding behind your back?"

She laughed and showed them a knapsack. "Your lunches!"

"You knew we'd want — how did you know?"

"Oh, we all have our secrets." Mother looked hard at the pillow in Neil's hand. He blushed and hastily put it back on the bed. "Have fun, boys."

"Do you suppose she's psychic?" Neil asked as they cycled down the broad graded road towards Weaver's Landing.

"I don't believe all that stuff. She's probably just a good detective."

"We should really have her in on this, whichever she is. She'd be good at it. It's the spookiest thing, hunting for clues a century and a half old."

They turned right at the river. Neil looked along the twisting narrow Number Two Highway connecting Toronto and Montreal. He tried to imagine what it would have been like when Alexander was alive. It would be a dirt road then, furrowed with wagon wheels and pitted with horses' hooves, with an occasional wooden house, most of them smaller than the merchant MacAlpine's, built along the way. The fields would be much the same, stone-fenced with the rocks that every turn of the plough uncovered. It was hard country to farm, glacial debris scattered atop the Precambrian Shield. It must have been even harder then, with hand-tools and horses. But this was as close to their precious New England as the Loyalists could get, and here they had settled, doggedly picking stones, scratching to free what there was of fertile soil.

"Look, Neil. Neil! They've started on the house next door."

Neil looked round vaguely. For a few moments he had really been back there. It was a shock to see the gas-pumps, the ramshackle corner store with its unpainted wooden sides held together with rusted metal signs telling one to 'Drink Coca-Cola', instead of MacAlpine's fine store of a hundred and fifty years before.

Jamie had jumped off his bike and propped it against the budding forsythia bush in the MacAlpine yard. Neil followed him slowly. The cellar was a dusty, uncompromisingly empty hole. What could there be to find down there?

"Come on, Neil." In wild excitement Jamie ran past

the MacAlpine place to the next-door lot, where the house-moving crew was starting operations.

Big holes had already been driven through the cellar wall just under the main flooring and then square beams, over a foot thick, had been run through from front to back of the house. As the boys watched, the beams were slowly raised by enormous jacks, half an inch, an inch. Slowly the whole house was being lifted off its foundation like a slice of pie on a server. When it was high enough the horse-shoe shaped carrier of the giant mover would slide under the beams and accept the whole weight of the house, ready to take it to its new home. There it would be slowly replaced on a new concrete basement, shaped exactly to fit the old house.

Jamie knew that brand new roads had had to be constructed and miles of electric and telephone lines moved, simply to save the five hundred or so houses from the area to be flooded. He looked up at the tires of the giant mover and put his hand on one of them. The size. The power. He couldn't wait to get through school and get on with the business of living.

"Watch it, young man," one of the tough tanned men, that Mr. Hartshorne had brought up from New Jersey, called down from the top of the rig. "Better keep out of the way. We'll be moving her in soon."

"Is it okay if we explore the cellar next door?"

"Why not? I'd feel a lot safer with you down there." The man laughed.

"Did you do that on purpose?" Neil asked.

Jamie nodded, a broad grin on his freckled face. "If we'd gone right in there and ignored the mover they'd have wondered what we were up to. Wow, I wish I could drive that thing." He turned away regretfully.

The cellar was deep, but at the back worn stone steps led down from where the kitchen garden had been. They climbed carefully down and looked around. It felt very odd, the world abbreviated to a sequare of grey sky and four stone walls. It smelt damp and felt like a dungeon.

"There's nothing here," said Jamie after a tour of the walls. "Unless it's buried." He looked dubiously at the rockhard dirt floor. "It's so empty. There really isn't anywhere to hide anything."

Neil sat down on the cold steps and shut his eyes. He tried to imagine Alexander MacAlpine with something to hide, something he intended to use later. Though why hadn't he? That was another puzzle.

He got up slowly and ran his hand over the wall. "Behind a stone. If there is anything here it's *got* to be behind a stone."

They explored the walls, prying at stones until their nails were cracked and their fingers felt dry and sore.

"Oh, it's useless. We must be wrong. The stones are as tight as can be, except right at the top where they poked the house-moving beams through."

"Do you suppose . . . " Jamie scrabbled at the wall with his hand and feet. "Ow. Give me a leg up, Neil." Astride the broken gap at the top of the cellar wall he looked down. "These stones are quite loose, all right." He wiggled one out as he spoke, and it slipped and slid down into the cellar with a crash, right at Neil's feet.

"Well, wait till I get out of here, dum-dum. I don't have a hard hat on." Neil ran across the cellar and up the steps. By the time he had walked around to the front of the cellar Jamie had climbed off the wall and was exploring the next gap.

"It's useless, Neil. Look. There are lots of gaps between the stones, damp courses, I suppose. But there's no way of getting anything out, even if we knew where to look."

"Yeah. We'd need X-ray eyes." Neil turned away gloomily.

"That's it," Jamie shouted. "You've got it, Neil. Look, anything that's lasted in this damp climate would just have to be in a box — a metal box, wouldn't it?"

"Yes, I'll buy that. But . . . ?"

"You know those metal detectors they use in Hydro?

For tracing buried lines and avoiding telephone cable and gas lines?''

"Wow. Do you suppose Dad would . . . ?''

"We can always ask him.''

"It's a terrific idea, Jamie. But let's not wait till tonight. Let's bike down to Cornwall and find Dad now. If he's willing to help us he could get a detector out of stores today and we could try it out tomorrow, when he's home. He'll never let us touch it ourselves. And tomorrow's Sunday. It's our only chance.''

The temporary office of the Power Project on the west side of Cornwall was a bustle of activity. A secretary told them that their father was expected in about an hour, so they sat on the fence around the parking lot to eat their lunch and then wandered into the reception area to wait for him.

Jamie was instantly absorbed in the charts and progress report graphs that hung on the walls. Neil wandered restlessly around. The atmosphere bothered him. It was too noisy and hurried, and he couldn't get excited over the graphs, the way Jamie did. Along one wall was a model of the whole project, from Iroquois to Montreal. That was more fun. He tried to imagine himself scaled down to its size. He found Weaver's

Landing. Every tiny island and rock in the river was marked. It was better even than Mrs. MacAlpine's survey map. What was that name over there? He bent over the model in sudden excitement.

"Jamie. Sss. Jamie! Over here."

Reluctantly his brother detached himself from a graph showing how many cubic yards of concrete had been poured every week since the Power Dam was started.

"What is it, Neil?"

"Jamie, just look at this model," Neil whispered. "Don't shout about it. Just look at that island downstream from Weaver's Landing. See the name. Shush!"

Jamie gave a gasp and looked across at his brother, his eyes shining. "Treasure Island!"

"It *can't* just be a coincidence. Can it?"

They were still poring over the model when their father strolled up.

"Hi, guys. I heard you were looking for me. What's up?"

"It's a secret project, Dad. We can't tell you about it here."

"But we need your help."

"Mmm. I make it a rule never to go into things blindfold."

"We *will* tell you. Honest. But just not here. Please trust us, Dad."

"Well, okay. What do you want?"

"Could you borrow one of the metal-detecting things from Hydro and help us run it over Mrs. MacAlpine's cellar tomorrow?"

"Mrs. Mac . . . there's nothing down there but waterpipes."

"Not the new house. The old one."

Their father opened his mouth.

"Oh, don't ask questions. Please. We'll tell you all about it tomorrow. Honest."

He looked down at them, hesitating. But Neil could see the twinkle in his eyes and knew that they had won.

Chapter Four

As the first pale light shone through the chintz curtains of the dormer window into Jamie's eyes he rolled over with a grunt. Neil woke up with a start and looked at his watch.

"Come on, Jamie. It's after six o'clock. Jamie. Get up."

"It's too early. It's Sunday. Nobody's up." Jamie pulled the pillow over his head and burrowed under the covers.

"That's the idea, dum-dum. The treasure-hunt, remember? We don't want the whole world watching us. Do get going. I'll wake Dad. We can be off in ten minutes if we don't bother washing."

"You mean we're actually going treasure-hunting without breakfast?" Jamie was dismayed, as, still half-asleep, he was hustled into his clothes and out of the house.

"I sympathize completely, son." Father ran a hand over his stubbly chin. "But when your brother gets an idea in his head he's ruthless, both to himself and to any one else who is unfortunate enough to get involved. Anyway if we wake your mother or Mrs. MacAlpine at this hour we'll really be in for it, so let's get going without complaint. Maybe you'll find a chocolate bar in the glove compartment."

They parked off the road on the old MacAlpine lot. Father quietly opened the trunk. Everything was very still. The houses showed shuttered and curtained faces to the deserted highway. A mist was rising clammily off the river, hiding the sun. Far downstream in the old canal a laker hooted dismally as it chugged slowly up the river. Every pebble under their feet echoed in the damp air like gunshots.

"Leave the trunk open. It'll make an ungodly noise if you slam it now." Father whispered. "Now, boys, how do we get down?"

They showed him the steps at the back, and with his hands full of equipment he walked carefully down the stone slabs, now slippery with mist.

"I just brought the earphones and the detector. I presume you don't need a permanent record." He slipped on the headphones as he spoke, adjusted a control, and then, holding the wand out in front of him began to pass it slowly to and fro across the stone walls.

"You look as if you were vacuuming," Neil laughed.

"He can't hear you, silly. Just the hum in the earphones," Jamie said knowingly.

"Nothing on that wall. Want to try?" Dad took off the headphones. Jamie grabbed the set and began to sound along the south wall. Nothing there. It was Neil's turn. He looked curiously at the equipment.

"What am I supposed to be listening for?"

"A change of pitch and intensity — higher as you get near metal. Don't worry. It's quite unmistakable. Off you go."

But when Neil had been over the west wall and Father had taken over the headphones again to listen along the north wall, they had not heard a single unusual sound.

"Well, I guess you kids must have been wrong after all. I'm sorry, Neil. Your idea certainly seemed logical."

"I suppose the equipment is working okay?"

Father took a jack knife out of his pocket and wedged the open blade between two stones. He held out the headphones and waved the wand around. They all heard the scream as it approached the steel blade.

Neil sighed heavily. A soft rain was beginning to fall, clinging to clothes and hair. Jamie shivered. "I'm starving. Can't we go and have breakfast now?"

"Better go, Neil."

"Just a minute, Dad. I know I'm right. It has to be here. Let me think." Neil sat on the stairs, his head in his hands, trying to imagine himself in a dark cellar, flickering lamp in one hand, box in the other. Some place that was safe. That he would remember and could come back to. He could just see Alexander coming carefully down the stairs.

"The stairs! That must be it. Dad, Jamie! Under one of the stairs. It would be easy to remember without marking, no matter how long he had to wait. And we never tested the stairs."

He grabbed the headphones and with trembling hands passed the wand to and from across each stair. The first. The second. The faint hum in his ears increased to a whine. The third. The whine changed to a scream. The fourth. It faded. Go back again. Steady now.

He looked up at the others. "Here, Dad. Behind the third step. It has to be here." He couldn't stop grinning.

They crowded around, the rain falling unnoticed on their necks and backs, as Father knelt and carefully slid the blade of his jack knife around the crack where the third riser joined the step above.

"Easy. I'm going to break this blade if I'm not careful. The stairs must have settled. It's very tight."

"It's coming, Dad. I can see a crack at the side now. Keep going."

Slowly, painfully, with fingernails and the jack knife, they eased the stone forward. The hiding-place had been well made. The stone was about eighteen inches wide and the height of the riser. Its sides had been slightly bevelled so that it couldn't accidently be pushed through into the space behind.

"This must have been done when the house was built." Father grunted, as he pushed the slab to one side. "Eighteenth century idea of a safe, I suppose. Your find, Neil. Go ahead."

Neil took a deep breath and put his arm into the dark gap between the stairs. He felt around, his fingers imagining the cold smooth touch of metal. He found something. It felt like a rough old brick. He pulled it forward, his heart sinking. But it was all right. He hadn't realized what a hundred and fifty years in a damp cellar would do. The metal was rough and blistered with rust, and the copper fastenings were stained green with verdigris. He blew gingerly at the stone-dust and cobwebs. They clung, damply. When he brushed his fingers across the top of the little box the rust came off red on his hands.

"We found it. It was really there. Oh, Dad!"

"Take it easy, Neil. Let's wrap it in my handkerchief, and for pete's sake carry it carefully. It looks about ready to fall apart. Now let's get out of this infernal rain."

"And get some breakfast," Jamie put in cheerfully. "Let me carry the detector, Dad. Gee, it's neat. It really does work, doesn't it?"

Neil sat in a daze, the precious box in his lap, while Dad drove up the road, now slippery with rain, and Jamie rattled on about detectors.

Mrs. MacAlpine turned in astonishment and dropped the kitchen poker as they trooped in the door. "Mercy me, what have you all been up to. You're drenched through and that dirty! Fancy going off without a word and no breakfast either. You must be fair clemmed."

"We've got it." Neil cut triumphantly through the chatter. He put the box down carefully in the middle of the kitchen table and folded back the handkerchief. "It's Alexander's box, Mrs. MacAlpine," he announced proudly and then sneezed.

"Losh!" Mrs. MacAlpine wiped her hands on her apron and reached out to touch the box. Neil sneezed again and she drew back her hand resolutely. "Well, it's waited for a century and a half. It can surely wait an hour more. Boys, you go on up and get out of those filthy clothes and jump into a hot bath this minute. By the time you're down I'll have a good hot breakfast on the table." She looked hard at father. "You're pretty wet yourself, Mr. Anderson and awfu' dusty."

"Er, yes. You're so right, Mrs. MacAlpine. Off you go, boys. I'll go and get cleaned up too."

By the time the boys were bathed and dressed and down in the kitchen their mother had joined them, her dark hair smoothed back, her face as calm as if they ate breakfast every day with a treasure box in the middle of the table.

Finally the last cup of coffee was drunk, Mrs. MacAlpine cleared, and Neil breathed a sigh of relief.

"Your property, Mrs. MacAlpine." Their father looked across the table eagerly. "Do you want to . . . ?"

"Please go ahead, Mr. Anderson."

Father prised carefully around the corroded hasp of the box with his knife. He worked slowly, his big fingers gentle. The others watched, holding their breath. There was a sudden snap. Scales of rusted metal fell to the handkerchief. Father lifted the lid. The hinge squeaked protestingly.

As the box opened they all came to their feet, leaning over the table.

"What is it?"

"Just a piece of paper."

"And a little bag."

"The treasure? It's awfully little."

"It's rawhide, I think. Hard to tell with all this mould."

"Maybe it's diamonds!"

"Couldn't be diamonds. There are no diamonds in Ontario, silly."

"If you get out of the light we'll have a look." Father opened the bag and spread the contents on the table.

"A root . . . some pebbles . . . a few little bones. It's a joke. Just a beastly practical joke!" Jamie was disgusted.

"It can't be." Neil felt heavy with disappointment. "Nobody plans a joke that nobody's going to see. Who was to know we'd find the box? It's *got* to mean something."

"What do you think, Madeleine?"

Their mother touched the objects delicately. "I'm sure you're right, Neil. It means something. But what it has to do with treasure, I don't know. This root — it looks like juniper — see how it's twisted. It's almost the shape of a person. The pebbles . . . they just look like pebbles to me. Nothing precious, Jamie, I'm afraid. The bones are bird bones, of course. I think an owl. It doesn't help much, I'm afraid."

"It's funny, the inside of the box isn't rusty, but that little bag is covered with red, where it isn't mouldy." Neil rubbed the bag with his finger and showed it, reddened.

"Mmm. Looks like red ochre. Maybe the paper will cast some light on the mystery. It's going to be hard to handle without spoiling. We mustn't ruin it by being in too much of a hurry. Gosh, my hands are filthy." Father got up to wash at the kitchen sink. "Madeleine, how can we stop that paper from falling apart?"

"A couple of sheets of glass would be the thing, Andrew. Have you got anything that would do, Mrs. MacAlpine?"

"No, I cleared out all the bits of junk from the old cellar before we moved."

"Never mind. I think I can find something." Mother ran lightly upstairs. It seemed ages to Neil, as they sat staring at the strange objects on the table, before she appeared again.

"I think these will do. I borrowed them off the photographs of you boys. I'll get them re-glazed next week. This is no time for sentiment. Here you are, Andrew. And some masking tape."

Gingerly Father unfolded the creased brown-spotted paper, smoothed it onto a sheet of glass and pressed the other sheet on top. "Tear me off the tape, will you, Madeleine?" He sealed all the edges of the glass with tape and then laid it down for them all to see. "There we are. We'll look pretty silly if we've reverently preserved a nineteenth century grocery list."

"It's funny writing. It's all speckly and scratchy, and it's got loops and squiggles over some of the words. What's on the other side, Dad?"

"A kind of picture, very roughly drawn."

"It's a map. Jamie, we were right. It's a treasure map!"

"I don't see how we could find anything with that, Neil. Just an outline that could be an island, with a cross up at one end. It's no sort of a shape, really. Could be any one of a hundred islands."

"Maybe the writing is instructions. Can you read it, Dad?"

"Beyond me. How about you, Madelaine?"

"I should be able to. I read an awful lot of old manuscripts when I was studying American history. The writing's okay, anyway." Mother looked up from the paper. "I mean it's perfectly characteristic of early nineteenth century writing. It's badly foxed, that's these brown blotches. I'll have to guess a bit. It says . . .

'The Place where Bruce McIntosh and I found the Indian Treasure, as near as I can Recall it, the Map and the Box of Treasure We Found being Lost at the Bottom of the Longue Sault Rapids, when we Overturned. God be Thanked We were not Drowned Ourselves. When I am Healed I will Return for the Rest. Then I will be Believed. Alexander MacAlpine.'"

In the silence that followed Neil could feel the spirit of the old Scot as tangibly as if he were in the room with them. He drew in a shaky breath. It was all true . . .

"But why didn't he go back?" Jamie protested. "It doesn't make sense. I mean it wasn't only the treasure. As he says, it was proving he wasn't a spy. You'd think he'd go back the first moment he could."

"I agree, Jamie. So that means he couldn't. How long did he live, Mrs. MacAlpine?" Mother asked.

"Let me see, now. Jock was born in 1840 and I know Alexander died when he was a wee bairn. So he'd have lived thirty years or thereabouts after the battle."

"Jamie's right. It doesn't make sense. He stayed right here, at Weaver's Landing, running the general store?"

"Aye. He was a canny merchant and made a fair bargain, they say, so they would have tolerated him, I suppose."

"I'm surprised he didn't leave and start again somewhere else."

"That would be hard. Merchandizing was all he knew. And him a cripple beside."

"A cripple! You never mentioned that."

"I guess I never thought of it. But I recall Alec's father Jock tell on how his father was a cripple."

"But a cripple couldn't go crawling round battlefields in the middle of the night. It's ridiculous."

"No, wait a minute, boys." Mother's voice was eager. "Suppose he wasn't a cripple *before* that night. What does it say in the note? When I am Healed. . . . That's it! Suppose he was wounded in the cross-fire, before the scout found him. Suppose he never did get better. Maybe some spinal damage. Doctoring must have been very rough and ready back then."

"You mean he had the secret of the treasure all those years and was never able to go back?"

"That's why he hung on. He must have been waiting for Jock to grow up. But he died when Jock was just a boy. And his secret died with him."

"Too bad the scandal didn't die too, but that's always the way of it, it seems."

"But what about Bruce McIntosh?" Neil asked. "He keeps coming up. He's in the note. He was Aexander's original alibi. You think he'd have turned up to support him and go back for the rest of the treasure, since Alexander couldn't."

"I don't suppose we'll ever know the answer to that one." Father leaned back in his chair and lit his pipe. "Well, Neil, you must be feeling very pleased with yourself. You set out to prove Alexander's story true and you've done it."

"Oh, Dad, that's only a beginning. There's still the treasure. *That's* the real proof. May Jamie and I take the map and try our hand at treasure-hunting? We know where to look, don't we, Jamie?"

"You bet we do."

"Why don't you trace a copy and leave the original with Mrs. MacAlpine. That's a historic document, you know. Where are you planning to go."

"Well," Neil and Jamie looked at each other. "It's kind of a secret."

"That's fine. If you're exploring in the Rapids section you'll be okay. There's a cofferdam right across from the shore to Long Sault Island, diverting the river into the South channel. You can explore in the dry. But if you want to look at the islands upstream you'll have to be very careful. Life jackets at all times. The currents are very powerful with the whole river flow being compressed into the one channel. Do you promise?"

"Yes, Dad. We promise."

"I sure hope this map is accurate. And I wish it would stop raining. Do you realize we've only got five and a half days left out of this vacation!"

CHAPTER FIVE

"This is stupid, Neil. We've wasted two whole days. It's no fun." Jamie stood on the eastern tip of Treasure Island, throwing twigs into the river and watching the current whisk them away downstream. Out of sight around the bend they could hear the rumble of the New York Power Authority bulldozers working on the Long Sault Dam. Treasure Island was still and barren. Not so much as a bird.

Neil looked around with a sigh. Jamie was right. It was a rotten treasure island, just a hunk of weathered rock sticking out of the river, a few scrubby bushes clinging to meagre cracks. It didn't even look very much like Alexander's sketch.

"I'm bored with treasure-hunting," Jamie went on. "I vote we go down and see how the Power House is coming on. There probably isn't any silly treasure anyway."

"That's not the point, Jamie. I'm not really looking for treasure. Well, just a bit maybe. But mostly I want to find out the rest of the story for Mrs. MacAlpine. She's got the right to know what really happened."

"You've got the note and the map. What more do you want?"

"Oh, Jamie, there are still so many unanswered questions. Why didn't Bruce McIntosh come back and support Alexander's alibi? Why didn't he go back for the treasure? What *was* the treasure that was worth risking their lives over?"

"It's all so long ago, Neil. The Power Project is *now*."

"It's as real to me as if it happened yesterday. They were real people. And Mrs. MacAlpine is real, and so are her problems."

"Well, we're not going to solve anyone's problems on this hunk of rock, anyway. But you're really weird, Neil. Getting all worked up and acting like a detective in a hundred and fifty year old mystery! Maybe you'd better be an archaeologist or something when you grow up."

"That's enough sauce from you, young Jamie." Neil

spoke automatically. It was one of those moments in life when something goes CLICK and you know surely and completely what you're meant to do. Archaeology. Funny he'd never thought of that before. He'd talk to old Carruthers when he got back to school, see if he was getting all the right courses. He suddenly felt very happy. Just three days . . .

Three days! Jamie was right. They had been wasting their time here. One last look round and a scramble down the smooth rock face to the canoe. They paddled hard to shore, angling the bow upstream into the current. They hauled the canoe out of the water at Weaver's Landing and upended it on its trestles.

As they unlocked their bikes, which had been hidden in the bushes by the water, Neil looked across at Jamie, still red-faced and cross with his wasted morning. "Look, Jamie, I'm sorry. Let's bike down to Cornwall and see how things are going. And we'll just *look* at the islands as we go by, just to see if any of them are a bit like the one in the map."

Jamie cheered up and they rode off together. There was no wind and little traffic and they made good time past Farran Point and Dickinson's Landing.

"That's odd, Jamie. Listen."

"I don't hear anything."

"That's what I mean. We ought to be able to hear the rapids by now."

"Wow!" Jamie threw his bike down on the grass verge. "Come on. Remember? Dad said the Rapids had been de-watered. Let's go and see."

"Funny we never noticed it last time."

"We were in a hurry that day and it was windy too."

Just upstream of where the boys had stopped was the gate of Lock 21 of the old Cornwall Canal. They walked carefully across the top. The gates swayed and the water sucked and gurgled darkly beneath them. From the dyke which separated the canal from the river they could see the dried-up river bed, where for thousands of years the Long Sault rapids had raged.

Now it was a tumult of grey rock slabs, scarred and torn, upended at threatening angles, stones drilled through by the force of thousands of years of water plunging over them towards the sea. It looked like a cross between a battle-field and the ruins of an ancient temple. In a few deep spots pools reflected the sky. Most of it looked as dry and grey as if it had never seen water.

"It's super. Absolutely super."

"Just look at that rock over there. I bet that'd make the river-boat pilot's blood curdle. Do you suppose they had any idea what they were going over?"

"I should think they'd have turned right back. Just look at the razor edge on that big slab!"

"This is the most super place for beach-combing, Neil. We've only got three days left. Come on," Jamie pleaded. "I'm sick of treasure hunting and you know Mom and Dad'll make us stick together."

Neil hesitated. It was a rotten map. If Treasure Island wasn't the right place, then almost any other island in the river would fit. And there were dozens.

He made up his mind. "Okay. Let's beach-comb. You never know. We might get lucky and find the box Alexander and Bruce lost, the one with the real map and some of the treasure."

"Oh, you and Alexander! You've got a one-track mind."

"Well, we might as well beach-comb scientifically as not. Let's start exploring right up by the coffer dam and work our way downstream."

"I'll go along with that, so long as you let me keep any stuff I find."

"It's a bargain. And we've got three whole days, after all."

But on the Saturday before going back to school Mother put her foot down. "I've seen nothing of you the whole holidays. It's bad enough being a Project widow all year, but a treasure-hunting . . . what is the word for a mother with no children?''

''Try abandonee,'' Father suggested. ''Your mother's right, though. Take a day off with us. You've broken your back going over the bottom of the rapids and nothing to show for it but an old cannon ball.''

''Absolutely super,'' put in Jamie. ''Can I keep it on the front lawn at home? None of the guys have anything like it.''

''Well . . .''

''Better there than in his bedroom,'' Mother put in hastily, and Father chuckled.

''Take that glum expression off your face, Neil. I know it's tough, but it's not the end of the world. You'll have two or three weeks in the summer to go on looking before we flood the Rapids section of the river again.''

''I know, Dad. I just wish there was some more scientific way of going about it. There's just no way of covering every inch of three miles of river on your knees.''

''Why don't you ask around at school? I know you're not a science option yourself, but perhaps one of your friends might come up with a bright idea. In the meantime let's find out what your mother wants to do today.''

"The weather's perfect. I'd like us to go out and have an old-fashioned family picnic. Perhaps we could go over to the pioneer village place and see how it's coming along."

"Bus-man's holiday for you, Dad." Neil grinned.

"Oh, I don't mind. I'd like to show your mother the Memorial Garden. We've just finished the rough work. I think it's going to look really good. Bring your camera, Madeleine. There'll be some interesting inscriptions for your collection."

They picnicked on the short rough pasture grass above the future Upper Canada Village. Mrs. MacAlpine had done them proud. There was a hamper with hot ham patties wrapped in a white linen napkin, baked chicken legs and home-made rolls. There was plenty of fresh lemonade, and brownies and apples for dessert.

Jamie lay back on the stubbly grass with a sigh. "Mmm. That was good. School food from tomorrow night on. Two whole months of it." He groaned.

"Poor darling," Mother exclaimed. "I'll try and keep you supplied with cakes and things. I wonder if I ought to suggest to Mr. Johnson that he give you more to eat?"

Neil burst out laughing. "I'd like to see his face. The

food's fine, Mother. Well, it's okay anyway. Our Jamie's a bottomless pit."

"It's all very well for you. You don't even see what you're eating most of the time. Got your nose in a book."

Mother began to look worried again and then laughed. "Oh, you boys. Too much. Too little. But you both look healthy in spite of it. How about going down to explore?"

She reached out her hand and Father pulled her to her feet. Neil looked up at them, squinting his eyes against the pale April sun. He suddenly felt good all over. Boy, he was lucky to have such decent parents. Even Jamie wasn't bad when he was kept in his place.

He jumped up. "Race you down."

It didn't take long to look at the houses. These were buildings of historic interest which had been salvaged from the various villages to be inundated when the headpond of the power dam formed the new lake. Some of them were in bad shape, abandoned and almost falling down. But either on the giant house-movers, or by being taken apart and reassembled, they had been hauled up here to be saved for future generations to see. They sat forlornly in the pasture, doors and windows boarded up. The old Robertson place. The church. The schoolhouse. Crysler's Farmhouse.

Mother tried to peer through cracks in the boards across the windows.

"You'll just have to be patient," Father put in. "You won't believe how good it'll look in another year or so. The experts have been poring over these houses as if they were precious documents. They've analyzed paint samples, slivers of wall-paper and so on. Everything in the restoration will be as authentic as it's possible to be." He looked around the bare field. "There's going to be a miniature canal and lock system, with bateaux like the ones the earliest settlers used. There'll be a cloth factory run by water power and all the home industries — cheese-making, spinning, weaving, a blacksmith. I believe they're considering growing flax right here, so you can see the whole process from the beginning. Come on, Madeleine, I want to show you the Memorial Garden."

The boys followed behind. Mother seemed very excited, but it didn't look like much to them. Just a low stone and brick wall enclosing a bare patch of ground. Set in the wall, in a kind of mosaic, were gravestones, some so old and dilapidated as to be almost unreadable.

"It's not much of a garden. What's all the fuss about?" Jamie kicked a pebble across the dry ground.

"It will be one day. Give the Parks Department time.

We've only just got the wall finished. That's what I wanted your mother to see. You see, Jamie, we not only had to relocate all the families before the flooding and move all these precious old buildings, but we had to give consideration to the dead too. There were tiny little cemeteries scattered all along the river. Every village had its own. We arranged to have the remains properly reinterred inland and we collected the stones to set in this wall, which incidentally is made from bricks and stones of houses too dilapidated to save."

"That's keen! Tell me about how you dug up the graves." Jamie's eyes gleamed with interest. "Did you use bulldozers or just spades?"

Neil left them to it and wandered off to look for his mother. He found her photographing a stone commemorating the death of a little girl at the age of twenty months. He looked around at the other stones. So many of them died young. How come?

"Oh, Neil, it was just the same in the old New England cemeteries I used to explore. Typhoid, I suppose, or scarlet fever. But if they did survive infancy in those days, why, they just seemed to go on for ever. Just look at this, eighty-seven. And this, ninety-three."

"I thought science and medicine has increased our lifespan."

"Our *average* life-span at birth. Mostly by taking

care of infants and mothers. But if they did make it through childhood in those days I think they did better. Fewer stresses."

"Oh, come on, Mother. Wars, Indians . . ."

"Those are dangers, not stresses. You can do something about danger, even if it's only to run away. But a stress is something you can't seem to do anything about. That's what wears people out today."

"You mean things like pollution and the bomb?"

"Yes, those are stresses right now. Maybe we'll be able to do something really constructive about them in the future."

"Then they'll only be dangers?"

"Right."

"I wonder how exams qualify?"

"You can always learn your subject, so they're only dangers." They laughed and walked on.

"Here's one guy who didn't make it to the Methuselah category." Neil pointed out. "Look, he was only twenty-one. I wonder what happened to him?"

"The stone's so worn it's hard to read." Madeleine Anderson ran her fingers lightly over the inscription. "McIntosh. Well, that's common enough in this part of the world. It's right here they developed the McIntosh apple, you know. B..c.McIntosh Born something something 1792. D . . . must be died, November 11, 1813, ag . . aged twenty one."

"That name rings a bell. Where did I . . .?"

"There are dozens of McIntoshes in the United Counties."

"No, something else. What was it? I know, Mother! It just has to be." He ran his fingers over the worn stone. "B. Blank. Blank. C.Blank. Bruce! Remember, Mother. Bruce McIntosh. The friend who never came forward to back up Alexander's story. The man who never went back to find the rest of the treasure. I know why." He pointed triumphantly at the stone. "Just look at the date, Mother!"

They squatted down by the wall looking at the worn grey stone. "November 11th, 1813. The Battle of Crysler's Farm."

"They must have got separated," Neil whispered. He was back, imagining the cold wet dawn, the two men soaked and shivering from their drenching in the river, crouching bewildered in the ravine, American troops at their back, Canadian and British guns trained on them from across the bare winter fields. Sleet and a low mist. "Alexander picked up a stray bullet. The Indian scout found him and brought him in. But Bruce . . . he wasn't so lucky. I suppose he lay on the battlefield till it was all over, and the local people found him and buried him."

"So when Alexander used him as a witness he was already dead?"

"Only he probably didn't know it. And it would make the local people even more positive he had been lying, picking a dead man for a witness."

"What are you two doing?" Father and Jamie strolled up.

"Oh, communing with history," said Mother.

"And answering riddles," added Neil provocatively.

CHAPTER SIX

Letter from Neil Anderson to Andrew Anderson

Dear Dad,

Thanks for sending me those terrific aerial photographs and the flow charts of the Rapids section of the river. As you suggested, I took my problem to the guys in the Science Club. You wouldn't believe the response! They've made a really super model of the rapids out of plywood, using your photographs of the de-watered river-bed. They say the flow patterns agree very well with your charts. So far so good.

The only trouble is that they keep asking me questions to which I don't have the answers, such as where was Alexander's boat when it capsized, what was the weight of the box, and how much water was going down the river in the November of 1813. I ask you! So we've had to fall back on guess work.

Since Alexander and Bruce survived the accident in good enough shape to walk back to Weaver's landing in time for the battle, I figure they must have capsized above the rapids. I'm sure if they'd tipped over right in the rapids they'd have been battered to death or washed far downstream. As to the water flow all we know for sure is that the water level of the Great Lakes has dropped disastrously with the development of industry, so we can assume that there was much more water coming down the St. Lawrence a hundred and fifty years ago than there is today.

Anyway the guys showed me today what they're doing and it's really neat. They're dropping ball-bearings of different sizes into the model from different sections upstream of the Rapids, at different water flows, and marking how many lodge against what particular rocks and shelves. It's a slow job, but they swear they'll be finished by the summer holidays. They're making a really cool chart that'll show at a glance the most likely places to start looking. Isn't Science wonderful?

You know, Dad, Science used to turn me off, but the way these guys in the Club think is really something else. I guess there's a place for method as well as imagination, even in Archaeology. Especially in Archaeology, old Carruthers would say. By the way, he says I'm getting enough history, but I need some Geology, horrible thought. He told me there was some digging going on down at the Power Project. I thought he was putting me on, joking about the dams and dykes, you know, but he was really serious. Do you know anything about any archaeological digs down there, and what's it all about?

Jamie's really cheesed off that he's not old enough for the Science Club. Helping make that model would be right up his street. I told him that after all he'll get to help me actually look for old Alexander's treasure, but he wasn't a bit impressed. I get the feeling he likes the model better than the real thing.

Jamie and I send our love to you both. Jamie says to thank Mother for the chocolate cake, which he says was super. Exams start in two weeks. In a month we'll be home again. Don't flood the rapids till we get there!

Neil

P.S. It's strictly illegal, but the guys are making book on the location of Alexander's treasure. I'd better find it, or they'll really scrag me!

CHAPTER SEVEN

Neil and Jamie cycled down the road from the new town and east along the highway to where the coffer-dam diverted the whole flow of the St. Lawrence River from the rapids, through a cut in Long Sault Island, to the south channel of the river. They had cycled down this road for the first ten mornings of the summer holidays and home again, tired and discouraged, every evening.

"Well, today's the last day. Thank goodness for that. Honestly, Neil, *school* was less work! Tomorrow's the big bang. Wow, that'll be something!"

Neil looked up at the big dam. He imagined it bursting in two, the river greedily tearing at the dirt, forcing its way back into its accustomed channel. "We've got to find Alexander's box today. We've just got to.

Come on, Jamie." His voice was grim and Jamie looked at him curiously.

"You're taking it so darn seriously, Neil. It's only something to do. It'll be kind of interesting to see if the Science Club guys' charts work out, but good grief, you're acting as if it were the end of the world."

"It's not that." Neil took a deep breath and tried to control his frustration. "Don't you understand, Jamie. It's a question of finding the truth. Of undoing all that prejudice. Mrs. MacAlpine . . . it's all so unfair."

"Well, take it easy. I haven't noticed her complaining. You're getting all worked up over nothing. I think you mind more than she does."

Neil turned his back and walked across the top of the lock gates without answering Jamie. He felt all muddled inside, but there just wasn't time to stop and analyze his motives now. The last day. He scrambled down the side of the canal dyke and began to walk along the stony river bed, map in hand.

He stared at the map the Science Club had made for him, with its collection of red dots for likely spots and the penciled 'X's' which told of days of usless back-breaking work. He stumbled over a rock and put out his hand to save himself.

"Hey, watch where you're going, Neil. You'll break

a leg. Wait for me." Jamie scrambled down the dyke behind him in a shower of pebbles. "Neil, I'm sorry. I didn't mean to pick at you."

"Oh, it's okay, Jamie. My fault really. I guess I'm kind of edgy. There are just four places left on my map. And only one day." His voice trailed off and he looked from the map to the river-bed and back again.

"Well, come on. Let's get started." Jamie's voice was determinedly cheerful.

They picked their way downstream. It was clear to see where the main current had once flowed, the places where the rocks were scoured more deeply, where the ground was smooth, with few small stones or sand. Walking was easier along these smooth sections, and the boys left them only to avoid the huge uptilted rocks which had been thrust up in some remote era.

These upthrust slabs and pinnacles had been the true danger of the Long Sault rather than the actual speed of the water in its forty foot drop towards Cornwall. They were the gravestones of countless travellers, Indian, French, British, American, since the river started to flow.

It was under and around these massive obstructions that Neil's scientific friends had found that most debris tended to collect. For the past ten back-breaking days Neil and Jamie had scratched and dug. Their hopes had been raised at each chink of metal on metal, only to be dashed again and again. At each site Neil had marked the date on the rock and an 'X' on his map.

Now the map was dotted with 'X's', and there were four sites left to explore. Which one next? Which held the most promise? Neil looked at the map, made up his mind and pointed.

"There — that big slab."

"It sure looks promising." Jamie scampered ahead, while Neil pushed the map into his pocket and picked up the knapsack. As the mass of water had crashed against this slab it had been slowed down, so that small objects suspended in the current fell to the bottom, while larger objects that had been slowly rolling along the smooth bottom were also brought up short.

The boys found that they had to dig a mass of compacted sand and small debris away from the wedge-shaped gap before they could see anything.

"When we started out," Jamie panted, as he scraped at the rock with one of Mrs. MacAlpine's trowels. "I thought we'd just look around the rocks till we saw it. I never thought we'd be quarrying."

Neil didn't answer. His hands were bruised and one of his nails was torn. His trowel broke, but he went grimly on, pulling stones out of the way. Their theories were certainly right. They found, lodged right under the slab, the rusted fluke of an anchor, and there was all sorts of small stuff, a hinge that looked as if it had come off a farm gate, a number of ancient square-cut nails and a fine collection of pop bottles, probably dropped off the pleasure steamers that used to run the rapids.

"Maybe we should collect them and trade them in. It's amazing how many aren't broken. At least we'd be getting something for our work."

"Oh, come on, Jamie. Look at the time!"

"Well, you pocketed those nails, I noticed."

"That's archaeology. Square-cut nails are really old."

"I wonder where they came from."

"A ship that broke up, I suppose. The timber would rot away and the nails would just roll around on the bottom."

"Maybe that's what happened to Alexander's treasure-chest?"

"What's that?" Neil looked wearily across at his brother, blinking the grit out of his eyes.

"Suppose there isn't any chest, Neil, because it's all broken up. Suppose all this is for nothing."

"It can't be," Neil shouted. "It's here somewhere. I know it is." He went on scrabbling through the sand and pebbles compacted against the rock slab. The sun rose higher and beat down on their head and shoulders. The trees up on Long Sault Island shivered gently in the breeze, but down at the bottom of the river, protected by the canal dyke and the coffer-dam, there wasn't a breath of air.

"Oh, Neil, can't we stop and eat. I'm bushed."

Neil looked across at his brother. Sweat had run down Jamie's forehead and cheeks, leaving streaks in the grey stone dust that powdered his freckled crimson face. His red hair curled damply against his forehead.

Neil grinned reluctantly and stood up. "Ouch! Okay. There's nothing more here anyway. It *is* almost noon. Let's walk over to the next spot and eat our lunch there. I'm sick of looking at this particular rock."

Jamie groaned and stood up stiffly. "Okay. Where to, slave-driver?"

Neil looked at his map and pointed silently downstream. He stooped to scratch the date on the rock they had just explored. He marked another X on the map. Only three more. If they were all as tough as the morning's site they would never be through in time.

There was a tiny triangular patch of shade under the next rock and Jamie squatted down in it and began to eat ravenously. Neil pulled a sandwich out of the box Mrs. MacAlpine had prepared for them. It was his favorite chicken and gravy on home-made bread. He took a bite and began to chew. But all he could think about was that this was the last day, the last chance. . . His teeth felt all gritty and the inside of his mouth was so dry he couldn't swallow. He took a swig of milk from the thermos and ate a tomato, and then he began to poke around the new site.

He found an old steel knife, its handle disintegrated, which was better than bare hands. He began to pry and dig at the side of the rock.

"Neil?" Jamie's voice was cautiously polite.

"Hmm?"

"If you really don't want your sandwiches is it okay if I eat them?"

"Go ahead. I don't care." Neil heard a chink of metal against the knife point and reached his arm under the rock, his heart pounding. But it was only an old iron kettle, gone overboard from the galley of some long forgotten laker. He swallowed. The disappointment sat in his throat like a lump. He blinked his eyes and went on working.

The shadows grew long under the rocks. This made working cooler, but in the shadows it was hard to see. It was a world of harsh contrasts, blazing sun on scoured white rock and black impenetrable shadows.

Without talking they moved on to the next site. The

rocks changed from white to gold and then to rose, as the sun grew lower. The mosquitoes that infested the canal smelled them out and whined irritatingly around their damp heads and shoulders. It grew darker. Neil scraped and pried.

"Neil, isn't it nearly supper-time?" Jamie's voice was plaintive. Neil looked at his watch and his heart jolted. They were terribly late. He stood up and staggered. His knees were numb and his legs seemed to be made of string. The whole river lay in a pool of darkness, and in the west, in the green afterglow of sunset, the evening star was shining.

"Grab the knapsack, Jamie. We're going to have to hustle."

"I can't see a thing. We'll never get out of here," Jamie complained. "You're the one with the watch. You should have noticed the time. Dad'll be furious."

"Oh, come on and stop talking. We'll cut straight across the river to the canal dyke. It'll be easier walking."

He led the way over the tumble of rocks and pools to the dyke. "Just so we don't break an ankle in the hurry . . . Come on . . . There it is". They scrambled up to the flat top of the dyke. The mosquitoes rose in hoards from the still canal water to meet them. Slapping at their necks and shoulders the boys ran along the dyke to the lock-gate. It was horrible crossing in the dark. The gates swayed and creaked, and the water made threatening sucking noises as they scrambled across to the shore.

They dragged their bikes out of the bushes and pushed them up to the highway. Bicycling uphill to the new townsite was torture after a day spent on all fours. Neil felt as if his back was breaking in three separate places. His calves and thighs were cramped and his swollen hands could hardly grip the handle-bars.

"Are you okay, Jamie?" He forced the cheerfulness into his voice. Jamie groaned in reply. "Anyway the wind feels cool, doesn't it? And no mosquitoes." Neil spoke to cheer up his brother, but once he'd said it he realised it was true. The breeze through his wet hair and the dampness of his shirt was marvellous. He began to think about a bath and dinner. Not long now. He hoped Dad wouldn't be too mad. If only they'd been able to ride home triumphantly with the treasure. Then the tiredness and the lateness would be forgotten. If only . . .

They propped their bikes against the porch and fell into the house just as the clock was striking nine. Father looked up from the paper with a frown. Mother jumped up, took another look at them and changed her mind.

"Upstairs and into a bath, double-quick. Then come down in your dressing gowns. Mrs. MacAlpine has kept supper hot for you."

Nothing more was said until they were sitting at the table, eating beef stew and dumplings. Neil could hardly cut his meat, and his mother caught hold of his hand.

"Oh, Neil! I'll have to bandage these for you. Andrew, just look!"

"Are they very painful, son?"

Neil felt the tears rising in his eyes and he blinked hastily. Funny how kindness was worse than a scolding when you were really tired.

"It's all right, Dad. It wouldn't matter at all if only we'd found . . ."

"I know." His father's warm grip on his shoulder was comforting. "Did you explore all the sites?"

"Not the last one." Neil's voice broke. "No more light."

"And tomorrow the New York Power Authority floods the Rapids section. Eight o'clock on the button. I'm sorry, Neil. Really sorry. But win or lose you did a really good job. You gave it every ounce of your will and energy and that's what counts in the long run."

"Maybe it counts for me, Dad. But it doesn't help

Mrs. MacAlpine. It doesn't bring her any closer to the truth." Neil felt the taste of failure bitter in his mouth and he stared glumly at the table-cloth. All that work for nothing!

CHAPTER EIGHT

Jamie woke up suddenly. It was still dark in the attic bedroom, but in the pre-dawn glow coming through the dormer window he could see the shadow of his brother.

"Neil? What is it? What are you doing?"

"Pipe down, you idiot. You'll wake up the whole house. I'm just going to the bathroom. Go back to sleep."

Jamie rolled over in bed. There was a clean fresh summer smell drifting in through the open window . . .

When he next woke up it was to the smell of coffee and bacon. It was broad daylight. He sat up in bed and remembered. Today was the day of the big bang. It was the day they were going to blow up the coffer-dam at the head of the Long Sault Rapids, and reflood the rapids section of the river, now no longer to be rapids but a still pond behind the unfinished power dam. Gosh, it was exciting. And Dad had promised to take them down to watch the fun.

"Neil. Wake up! It's time." The hunched figure in Neil's bed didn't move and Jamie bounced out of bed and ran over to shake him. The shape disintegrated into a pillow and a rolled-up dressing gown. Neil was gone. What a dirty trick! I'll get you for this, he thought, as he scrambled into his clothes and pounded downstairs, stopping only to splash his face in the bathroom on the landing below.

"Neil, you stinker not to wake me," he shouted as he ran into the kitchen. His mother and father were already at the table, and Mrs. MacAlpine, neat and unruffled as ever, was dishing out bacon and eggs. It was a quarter past seven by the carriage clock on the mantel. They all looked up at Jamie in surprise.

"Neil's not down yet, Jamie. We thought you both were sleeping in a bit after yesterday's efforts."

"He's not upstairs, Mom. He left a dummy in his bed. Not that it fooled me, not for a moment."

"What on earth. . .?" Father went out onto the porch. They could hear his voice calling Neil. He came back. "His bike's missing. He must have just gone for a spin before breakfast."

"That doesn't sound much like Neil." Mother was doubtful. "He was so tired last night, and those hands."

"He must have left awfu' early, Mr. Anderson," Mrs. MacAlpine put in. "For I was down myself before six and there was not a soul stirring then."

"What could the boy be up to?" Father grumbled. He sat down at the table and started his breakfast. "Well, if he's not back before ten to eight I'm not going to hang around waiting for him. He'll just miss the flooding and that's all there is to it. Jamie and I will drive down and watch the big bang ourselves. Come on, Jamie, tuck in. There's not too much time."

Jamie began eating and then suddenly thought of something. He started to talk and choked violently.

"Take it easy, old chap. Moderation in all things. We do have half an hour."

Jamie struggled to talk and started coughing again. His mother hit him helpfully between the shoulder blades. Mrs. MacAlpine hovered with a glass of water. Presently he was able to gasp and get his voice back.

"Dad, I've just remembered something important. In the middle of the night. I woke up. Neil was getting up. He told me he was just going to the bathroom. So I fell asleep and didn't see him come back. Suppose he was really going down to the Rapids again?"

"In the middle of the night? Jamie, he wouldn't."

"Mom, he just might. He was awfully upset at not being able to explore the last site. Suppose he couldn't sleep. Or he woke up real early . . ."

"Andrew!" Mother gasped and jumped up from the table.

"Take it easy, Madeleine." Father put his arm around her. "Even if he did go down to the river he knows the schedule. He has a watch. There are warning klaxons at half an hour, fifteen minutes, and five minutes before blasting time. He's not stupid." He glanced at his watch and made up his mind. "Look, there's still almost half an hour to go. I'll just drive down and make quite sure he's clear of the blasting area. All right?"

Mother looked at him. Jamie saw that her eyes were huge and dark and her hands were over her mouth. Father shook her gently. "Stop worrying, Madeleine. It'll be all right, I promise you." He picked up his jacket from the back of the chair and felt for the car keys.

"What about me?" yelled Jamie.

"Well, come on if you're coming. I'm not waiting."

CHAPTER NINE

Neil let out his breath in a long sigh of relief as he pedalled down the road to the river. He glanced at his watch. Still too dark to see the hands. But a luminous glow in the east forecast the dawn of another clear day. It couldn't be much after four o'clock. He'd be able to get in nearly three hours work before biking back to the house and sneaking into bed in time to be woken up at the official time.

He chuckled to himself. That had been a nasty moment when old Jamie had wakened up. But he'd fooled him all right. He took an apple out of his pocket and ate it as he rode along. This morning he felt great. And lucky. He had this sure feeling inside him today, in the last place of all, he was going to find Alexander's treasure box.

He hid his bike in the usual place, crossed over the lock gate and ran lightly along the top of the canal dyke. This must be about the place where they had finished the previous night. He slid down the dyke side and cautiously picked his way among the boulders and rock shelves of the riverbed. His heart was jumping. Slowly, Neil, old man, he told himself. Slowly. He longed to get to the new site and start work, but it was still pitch dark down at the bottom of the river and the footing was tricky enough even in daylight. Can't afford to break an ankle now, he told himself. Look pretty silly lying down here with the water coming in. Carefully he crept along.

Here was the site of yesterday's work. Just a little farther. Yes, this was the place! He looked cautiously round. He was hidden from the coffer-dam by a bend in the river and from the downstream area by the bulk of Long Sault Island. Could he be seen from the shore? It would be too much to be hauled away before he'd had a chance to find the treasure.

He fished his flashlight out of his pocket and switched it on, keeping his fingers over the bulb. Carefully, keeping it low, he played it over the rock surfaces of the new site. He was in luck. The main obstruction was a huge rock slab, lying like a giant's tombstone across the bottom of the riverbed, the side near the north shore touching bedrock, the south end uptilted and supported by loose boulders. The slab itself would act as a shield to mask his activities from the shore, and he would be able to use his flashlight freely.

Neil took off his jacket, propped the flashlight up under the angle of the rock slab and began to clear away the debris that had collected in the angle between the slab and the river bed. He worked hard, lying on his stomach, his head and shoulders under the slab, scraping away with the handleless knife he had found yesterday. Nothing there. He was down to solid rock.

He wriggled out, blinking the sand from his eyes, and stretched. Ow, he'd been under there longer than he thought. The sky was quite pale now and shadows were beginning to appear along the riverbed. He looked at his watch. Five-thirty. Lots of time still, really.

The flashlight looked pale and ridiculous in the strengthening light. He switched it off and set it down on the top of a nearby rock where he would not forget it. It was a darn good flashlight, with a strong beam and a signalling button. Well, there was no danger of being betrayed by a flicker of light now. The strengthening light in the east only darkened the shadows under the slab and he couldn't possibly be seen. One more hour. He'd give it just one more hour before packing up and going home.

He poked cautiously at the boulders which supported the south end of the rock slab in its uptilted position. Then he gave them a good kick or two. They seemed perfectly solid. He lay down on his stomach again and began to scrape away the drift of dirt and junk around the base of the boulders. He could feel pebbles digging painfully into his ribs and his hands were starting to throb again. He'd cleared away all the loose junk and there was no sign of a box, no sign of anything, in fact, except for an old iron ring lying on the sand, crusted and bubbly with rust.

He had been so sure! Neil could feel the disappointment rising in his chest. He wanted to lie there under the rock and bawl. Nothing for all that work. Nothing but a stupid iron ring! All his frustration boiled up in an anger at the stupid ring and he reached out to grab it, to throw it as far as his muscles could throw.

He gave a gasp as a pain jolted clear up his arm into his shoulder. What on earth? He looked down, shocked by the pain and saw what had happened. He had reached out to snatch the ring and had pulled his arm back, hard, all in one movement. But the ring hadn't come away. It wasn't lying loose on the river silt as it seemed to be. The shadows had fooled him. The ring was part of something, something still deeply imbedded in a pocket of dried-up river silt. He had tried to pick up the whole riverbed in one snatch. No wonder his shoulder hurt. He swung his arm cautiously. Well, it wasn't dislocated, anyway. He laughed ruefully.

Then it hit him. He could feel the blood roar in his ears. He dropped to his knees and began to scrape frantically. A ring, attached to what? He dug with the old knife. The outline became clear under his fingers. An oblong. Perhaps eight by twelve inches. Not a very large treasure chest. But *still.*

He wiped the loose dirt from the top with his handkerchief. There were initials engraved in the metal. Hard to see. He traced them with a finger. "A MacA." This was it, at last! He pulled at the ring. The box didn't budge.

Neil frantically wiped the sweat from his eyes and looked at his watch. Six o'clock. Two hours, and then all this would be under water. And he must be gone long before that, or Mother would worry, and as for Dad, wow!

He took a deep breath and lay down again, painstakingly sliding the knife down the sides of the box, digging away at the silt, hardened by a summer's exposure to the sun. He found that he could use the knife like a chisel, hammering it with a stone. He banged away. It was sticking on one side only now, the side right up against the boulders that supported the great slab. There was just no way he could get the knife in behind there. Nothing left now but brute force. He put his fingers through the ring and pulled. If the ring gave way now he was really sunk. He held his breath. How deeply would the rust have eaten after a hundred and fifty years of river bottom? He felt the box stir slightly under his hand. The ring held firm. But it was too small. He could only get three fingers through it and that wasn't enough of a grip. What was the time now? Six-twentyfive. He must hurry, or he'd never be back in bed by getting-up time. Come on Neil. Think. . .

He wriggled out from under the slab, undid the belt of his jeans, slipped the end through the ring and fastened the buckle. He'd have to stand up, to pull the box up as well as forward. How could he get the maximum leverage? He tried a couple of positions and finally settled for standing, one foot on the ground about a yard in front of the box, the other foot braced against the side of one of the boulders supporting the big slab. He wiped his hands dry on his pants, reached down and grasped the loop of leather belt in both hands.

Steady. He braced his feet. Now . . . His arm muscles shuddered at the strain. He gritted his teeth. He could feel, like a sixth sense, a faint stirring through the leather loop. He pushed his foot harder against the boulder and straightened like a spring, his whole body cracking with the effort.

Suddenly, smoothly, like a tooth out of its socket, the iron box came free. The foot that was braced against the boulder, suddenly with no work to do, flew up, and Neil fell back with a jolting thud. Less than a second later the iron box, swinging in an arc in its loop of leather, hit him on the side of the head. Just before he passed out Neil was aware of a tremendous noise, above and around him. It was like an earthquake. The world was nothing but noise and dust.

When Neil came to his senses it was the pain that he was most aware of. There was no noise now. No dust. Everything was very quiet and still. Had he dreamed it? He lay on his back, frowning up at the sky. Overhead a redwing sang with piercing shrillness. A long way off he could hear the faint rumble of bulldozers. The sun was hurting his eyes. He moved his head away. Ow! It ached. The sun? The sun shouldn't be in his eyes. The sun should barely be over the horizon. Something was very wrong.

He lifted his left wrist and brought it close to his eyes. The figures danced and swam. He blinked and willed them to stay still. The crystal was cracked. That just made it harder. Ten to seven? Seven? He was supposed to be somewhere at seven. He could remember that, even though his head ached so. Ten to seven. He watched the second hand sweep round the dial. It moved so fast he could hardly keep up with it. His mind was going so slowly. Hardly moving at all, in fact. It wasn't bad, lying here. The sun was warm and he felt so tired. He sighed and turned his head to the right, away from the sun-dazzle. As his eyes shut he glimpsed the box, close to his head, his right hand still twisted in the strap.

Memory flooded back. He struggled to sit up. He'd got to get out of here! He'd have to hurry. Almost seven o'clock. He was supposed to be back in bed at seven. Well, maybe they wouldn't be too mad with him. After all he had found the treasure after all, just as he knew he would.

As he moved the pain seized him again, an agony that seemed to begin somewhere in his left leg and spread through his whole body. He gasped and fell back, his vision darkening, his face cold and clammy. He tried to breathe slowly and deeply, until he could feel the blood returning to his head. Cautiously, without moving any of the rest of him, he raised his head and looked down.

It was so bad that at first his brain refused to take

it in. Neil found himself looking down the length of his body, noticing all the stupid little details, the rock dust that lay like talc all over him, the rent in the knee of his right pant leg. He forced himself to go on looking, down the length of his left leg, extended stiffly in front of him. To the great slab that had reminded him of a giant's tombstone. But it wasn't lying like a table across the riverbed any more. It was tipped over towards him, the whole enormous mass of it balanced across his left ankle bone.

He knew the truth now. He lay back, gasping, digging his fingernails into the palms of his hands. He felt so cold, and yet strangely the sweat was running down his face and neck into the collar of his shirt. Don't panic, Neil. Panic is the worst thing. Very carefully he tried to wiggle the toes of his left foot. Nothing there at all. No messages coming through. Maybe he didn't *have* a left foot any more. He couldn't see it. Digging the heel of his right foot into the ground and pushing with his hands, Neil tried to force himself backwards, away from the slab. The pain grabbed him again, harder this time.

When his head cleared and he looked at his watch again, a lot of time had gone by. It was ten after seven. He thought of Jamie and Mother and Dad. They'd be having breakfast now. Would the dummy in his bed fool Jamie? And for how long? Gee, that was a stupid thing to have done. Why hadn't he left a note? They wouldn't know where he was. They'd finish breakfast and then they'd drive down to the river and watch the dynamiting of the coffer-dam upstream. They'd watch the earth walls fall away and dissolve into the urgent water pouring downstream to fill up the river bed where he lay. How many feet? Ten? Fifteen? It didn't matter much. One foot would be deep enough.

The fear was tougher to take than the pain. It drove him into a sitting position, feeling around in the dust for the old knife. There it was. Perhaps he could dig under the rock slab. It wouldn't take much to pull him free. Maybe half an inch. That'd be all he'd need. Just a little half inch.

He reached down and began to scrape. Seven-twenty. Ten minutes later Neil was down to bed-rock. His ankle was immovable in its vice of stone. He threw down the knife and wiped his face. The fear grabbed him by the throat. He tried to push it away. He looked north along the shore. From his prone position he could see only the top of the canal dyke. It stretched, an empty grassy line, from left to right.

The silence was broken by a chattering sound. Neil looked up. Overhead a Power Authority helicopter chugged slowly upriver. If only he could signal. He felt in his pockets. Nothing there. The crystal of his watch? Too small to be useful. Then he remembered the flashlight. If only it hadn't rolled out of reach or been broken in the hail of stones and debris. He moved carefully around. There it was, sitting upright on the rock where he had placed it, all those hours ago, at first light.

He moved slowly, trying to reach it without stretching his trapped leg. Carefully now. His fingers grazed it. If it toppled now he'd never get it. He stretched another impossible half-inch and his fingers closed around it.

He lay on his back, panting, holding the flashlight up to the sky. Dot, dot, dot. Dash, dash, dash. Dot, dot, dot. Look. Oh, look, you idiot . . . The helicopter chuffed out of sight. Neil looked hopelessly along the dyke again. As he did so the scream of a klaxon tore through the quiet morning.

CHAPTER TEN

Neil's father drove fast down the highway and pulled up with a jerk at Lock 21 of the Cornwall Canal. As he switched off the engine a helicopter chuffed overhead and the klaxon near the coffer-dam upstream deafened them. He glanced at his watch.

"Seven-thirty. Half an hour till blasting time." He stood by the car and looked quickly around. "No sign of him."

"We usually hide our bikes in the bushes down there." Jamie pointed.

"Go and look, then. And hurry it up, Jamie. There's not that much time."

Jamie galloped down the slope, leaned over the bushes and shouted up. "His bike is here all right, Dad."

"Bloody little fool. What can he be up to? He must have heard the warning." He ran to the lock gate and peered downstream. "I don't see a sign of movement. Where would he be working, Jamie? Where were you last night?"

"Oh, miles downstream," Jamie said cheerfully. "You can't see it from here. It's round that bend." He pointed.

"Come on, then. Quickly." Father glanced at his watch and Jamie saw his lips tighten. He almost ran across the top of the lock gates, and, without waiting to see if Jamie was following him, set off at a gallop along the top of the canal dyke, his eyes scanning the riverbed as he ran. Jamie panted along behind. He wouldn't have believed the old man could move like that.

He tried to call out, but couldn't get enough breath. "Dad! Dad, stop!" He gasped and held his aching side. Father turned and came running back. "Over there." He pointed. "See that tilted triangular sort of rock. Well, that's where we were working yesterday evening."

"Do you know where the next place was?"

"No, Dad. Neil had the map. But downstream not too far."

Father muttered something under his breath and

stared down at the river bed, shading his eyes against the blinding glitter of the early morning sun. "These shadows. Blot everything out. Couldn't possibly see a person down there . . . Neil . . . ! NEIL!"

Jamie joined in the yell and then they listened, straining their ears. Nothing.

Father looked at his watch and started to run farther downstream along the dyke. Jamie turned to follow him and as he did so a flash of light caught his eyes. What was that? The sun on a broken piece of glass? No, there it was again. From the black shadow behind the huge rock way over across the riverbed. Three shorts. Three longs. Three shorts. And again. That meant S.O.S.!

"DAD!" At the tone of his voice Father turned and came running back. His eyes followed Jamie's pointed finger.

He drew his breath in hard. "Jamie, listen to me." He spoke fast. Jamie had never seen him look like this, his face muscles set, his eyes hard. "Stay on *top* of the dyke. No matter what happens you are not to budge. Understood? Right. The klaxon will sound twice more. If I'm not back by then, you are to lie down on top of the dyke, and stay there till after the blast. Okay?"

"Yes, sir." Jamie was beginning to feel scared. He watched his father run down the steep slope of the dyke and leap from stone to stone across the riverbed to the shadows on the far side. There was no signal flashing now, and Jamie could see no movement. Something bad must have happened to Neil. It couldn't be more than fifteen minutes to flooding time. Suppose . . . He gulped and pushed his hands into his pockets. It was silly the way they were trembling. Dad was here. He would fix everything. Nothing to worry about. But he remembered the expression on his father's face and shivered in spite of the warm sun.

Neil lay on his back with his eyes shut. He didn't hurt any more and he didn't seem to be afraid. His fingers on the button of the heavy flashlight lying across his chest continued to send out their signal . . . S.O.S. . . . S.O.S. He didn't know why. The helicopter hadn't returned and there was nobody else to see. A long way off in some other world he heard a shout. He didn't worry. Nothing to do with him. He lay on his back on the dry riverbed, his foot in a vise of stone, and waited quietly for the water to come. It was all rather like a dream. He sighed and his hand slipped off the flashlight . . .

This time the shout was close by. It intruded into his private dream world and bothered him. A pebble spun by, flicking his cheek. He frowned and opened his eyes. Who on earth? He blinked unbelievingly.

"Dad?" he whispered.

"Don't move." He could feel hands gently touching him, head, arms, legs. His eyes closed again. Why bother? In a few minutes it would all be over anyway. He was so tired.

He could hear his father's voice. He was shouting, shaking Neil's shoulders. Reluctantly he opened his eyes again.

"Neil! Neil, you've got to listen. Try to understand. I have to go back to the car and get the jack. I'll be back within ten minutes. I promise. You'll hear the fifteen minute klaxon while I'm gone. Don't let it scare you. I'll be back. Are you listening, Neil? I'll be back!" He was gone. Neil could hear the scrape of his boots on the rocks and the sudden skid of stones as he climbed the canal dyke side.

The minutes passed. The klaxon roared, scaring the redwings out of the bushes along the highway. Idly Neil looked at his watch. A quarter to eight. Right on time. The birds circled and swooped overhead and then dove back to the bushes. The sweep second hand spun round. It was going faster and faster. It made Neil's head spin. He shut his eyes. If only he could get back into that dream world where time didn't matter any more.

The scrape of metal on rock brought him back to reality with a jerk. His father was kneeling close by him. He could reach out and touch the rough tweed of his jacket. It was a comfortable sort of feeling. Father was pushing the car-jack under the tilted slab, close to the ground.

"It'll slip," he whispered.

"No, it won't." His father's voice was strong and confident. "Who's the engineer in this family?" Slowly he began to pump the lever of the jack up and down. Neil wanted to shout to him to go faster. The second hand on his watch was racing again, and they had to keep up with it or something terrible was going to happen. He struggled to sit up and as he did so his hand touched the strap of the box, still looped around his wrist. He pulled it towards him.

"Dad, I found the treasure."

"Damn and blast the treasure!" The blare of the klaxon seemed to echo his father's anger. He shrank back.

"Five minutes left." His father bent over him. His face was drawn and pale under the tan and his lips were tight. "Listen, Neil. I'm going to pull you out now and make a run for it. I don't have time to be careful. It'll hurt a lot. I'm sorry."

"Don't forget the treasure," Neil pleaded and

twisted the strap around his arm. His fingers closed on the rusty ring.

His father groaned and then stooped and pulled him back from under the rock. The pain was worse than before, worse than he could believe possible, and as his father threw him across his shoulder and started to run for the dyke, Neil could hear himself screaming.

He was dropped onto flat ground with a jolt, and at the same second the whole world became filled with a roaring crashing noise. The ground shook under him. It must be an earthquake, he thought feebly. He couldn't breathe. Someone was lying on top of him. He struggled weakly, and then the pain in his leg wiped out all the rest.

CHAPTER ELEVEN

Neil's world was beautifully cool and quiet. He stirred and felt smooth sheets and pillows. He opened his eyes. He was lying on his back in bed in a small green-painted room. His left leg was suspended in the air in some complicated apparatus that ran over a frame at the bottom of the bed. He puzzled over this and then remembered. His trapped leg. The flooding. The treasure. Lost for ever now, he supposed, under the St. Lawrence water. He'd done everything wrong, every last thing. He groaned and moved restlessly.

Someone was sitting in an armchair by the tall narrow window. "Mother?" he croaked.

"Neil, dear. How do you feel?"

"Okay, I guess. Thirsty."

She brought him a glass of water with a curved straw.

He found he could sip quite comfortably lying on his back.

"My ankle. Is it going to be okay?"

"Don't worry, Neil. The doctor says it'll take some time. You'll probably have to spend most of your vacation in that thing. But you should be able to go back to school in September in a walking cast, and it really will be as good as new.

"Thanks a lot." Neil laughed ruefully. "Mother, are you and Dad awfully angry with me? I really fouled things up. But I never meant to."

"Oh, Neil, we're so thankful to get you back alive and in one piece. No, we're not angry. Upset, perhaps. It was a crazy thing to do, Neil, and not a bit like you."

"I know, Mother. But I fully intended to be back in bed by seven."

"On the principle that what your parents don't know won't hurt them?" His mother's smile took the sting out of the remark.

Neil laughed. "Ouch! When you put it that way it does sound pretty sneaky. At the time it really felt like the right thing to do. You see, I had this kind of obsession about clearing the MacAlpine name. It's as if finding the truth about that was the most important thing in the whole world. I guess that sounds pretty silly. Anyway, it's no good now. I fouled it all up with that stupid accident. And now Alexander's box is back at the bottom of the river.'' He could feel the disappointment swelling in his throat. He swallowed and then saw his mother's expression.

''Mother? The box . . . ?''

''Yes, Neil, it's safe. Your father told me you had that thing in such a tight grip he couldn't pry your hand off it. In fact they couldn't get it away from you till you were in the hospital and they'd given you a shot of pain-killer.''

''It's safe? The box is really safe? We did it!''

''Take it easy now. Your father's got it. He and Dr. Williams will come in and talk to you about it when you've had a chance to rest, say, in a couple of days.''

''Dr. Williams? A doctor?''

''No. An archaeologist from Toronto. He's down here on some kind of digging expedition. He's pretty excited about your find. Now that's all I'm going to tell you for now. You need your rest. Jamie'll be in to see you later.'' She kissed him on the forehead and was gone.

Neil lay back, his thoughts scurrying around in his mind. He'd made it! They'd found Alexander's box. Wouldn't Mrs. MacAlpine be pleased. And the guys in the Science Club. They'd be thrilled that their theories were right after all. But what was all this about an archaeologist? He'd have to ask Jamie. Mother said Jamie'd be in soon.

It seemed an eternity before the red hair and freckled face of his brother poked around the corner of the door.

"Oh, there you are at last."

"Is it all right to come in?" Jamie looked in awe at the apparatus on Neil's leg. He tiptoed elaborately across the room to the bed and stood there awkwardly.

"Neil, are you really all right?"

"Of course I am, you owl. It's only a busted ankle."

"I thought you were going to die." Jamie gulped and looked down at his feet.

"Hey, there, Jamie. I'm fine. Honest. Now for pete's sake sit down and tell me what happened. How did you find me?"

"We saw your flashlight signals. Gee, you were smart, Neil." He looked shyly at his brother. "Dad made me stay on top of the dyke. When he went for the jack I thought he'd never get back in time. Neil, you should have seen him run! And he just sort of bounded across the river with you on his shoulder. And the dam was blown up right on time. It was terrific. I wish you'd seen it. I mean . . ."

"I know what you mean." Neil laughed. "Go on."

"The water came down so fast. We couldn't see the

coffer-dam from where we were on top of the dyke, but we saw the earth being blown up into the air, and then this huge sort of gush of water came pouring around the bend and down over the rapids. It just seemed to fill up in no time at all." Jamie's voice faded. He licked his lips and looked at his brother.

"It's okay, Jamie. It's all over. I'm here, aren't I?"

"Yeah, I guess. Gee, I'm glad, Neil."

"Believe me, so am I, Jamie! Now tell me all about the treasure. You know when I woke up I thought I'd left it behind. Life's flattest moment."

"I don't know much about it, Neil. This Dr. Williams is awfully excited about it, but I can't think why. It isn't as if . . ."

"As if what? Out with it, young Jamie."

"I promised Dad I'd wait and let him tell you about it himself. He'll kill me if I don't."

"Oh, come on. I can't wait!"

"I've got to go now, Neil. Dad's picking me up on his way home from work. 'Bye."

Neil felt that if he had something to throw he would have thrown it. Hints were worse than nothing. How was he going to wait through the next two days?

Somehow the time passed and the afternoon visiting hours of the second day arrived. He heard the footsteps outside his door and his father came in followed by a stranger, carrying the box. Neil's eyes were riveted on it, this box that had been the cause of so much trouble over the years. . . .the death of Bruce McIntosh, the crippling of Alexander and the ruin of the name of MacAlpine, and now very nearly his own death.

It was a very small treasure chest, not much bigger than an ordinary cash box, to have caused so much trouble. It had been cleaned up and Neil could see that it was made of iron with bands and hasps of brass. It didn't seem to be very heavy either, judging from the way the man was holding it.

"Neil, this is Dr. Williams, from the Royal Ontario Museum."

"Well, you've created quite a stir with your find." The man had a quiet, rather dry voice. Neil looked at his face for the first time. He was quite young, which somehow surprised him. Why should he have thought of archaeologists as being old? His mouth and chin were hidden by a bushy fair beard and blue eyes twinkled out of his tanned face.

"How do you do, sir." Neil spoke automatically and then his curiosity got the better of him. "How did you . . . I mean where did you hear about the chest?"

"We were right here in Cornwall. Some students from the University of Toronto and myself have been making what you might call a last-ditch dig on one of the islands just upstream of Sheek Island. We had strong reasons to believe that we might find the remains of an ancient Indian culture. There's never enough money for all the places one wants to dig, but when we realized that this would all soon be under water for ever, we scratched together the funds."

"As you know, Neil, Hydro is clearing off all the surface vegetation from the areas that will be under water, so that we'll have a clean lake for swimming and boating," Father explained. "So as we skimmed across the island with bulldozers, Dr. Williams and his diggers have been going along behind looking for clues."

"With precious little success, too." Dr. Williams laughed ruefully. "Just enough to whet our appetites. I know we're on the right track. But there's been so little time. With the completion of the Power-dam and the flooding of the whole area next summer it's now or never."

"But what's all that got to do with Alexander's treasure?"

"Suppose you look at it yourself." Dr. Williams brought the box over to the bed. "It's a bit grimy still. Could you get something, Mr. Anderson?"

Neil's father spread a towel on the white bedspread

and Dr. Williams carefully put the box down on it. Neil reached out and touched the box. It was hard to believe that it was indeed real. He had struggled so hard to believe in Alexander, to believe in the box. And here it was.

"May I open it, Dr. Williams?"

"Go right ahead."

The lid was stiff and Neil had to struggle to get it open. It was awkward not to be able to turn his body. He fought it for a moment and then the lid came open with a protesting squawk. He blinked in surprise and disappointment. It was like the other little box they'd found in the cellar. Just a sheet of birch-bark. A dried-up leather bag. Some shards of poetry. . . . No gold. No precious stones. He couldn't find anything to say.

The young archaeologist leaned eagerly over the bed, pointing. "See the leather gasket around the inside of the lid. It was a piece of luck that Alexander had a box like that to put his findings in. When it fell in the river the leather would have swelled. It made an air-tight seal . . . Absolutely air-tight."

"But, sir. That's not treasure. It's just a collection of . . ." He stopped.

"Of junk?" Dr. Williams laughed. "Don't you believe it. Far from it. Oh, I don't doubt Alexander must have thought so. He must have been furious at getting so little for his trouble. He probably imagined for the rest of his life the gold and jewels lying out there on the island beyond his reach. But treasure isn't always gold and jewels, you know."

Neil blushed. "It isn't?"

"No, indeed. Somehow Alexander came into possession of this map from the St. Regis Indians." Carefully Dr. Williams lifted the piece of birchbark from the box. "See the markings? Very faint. But we've had it photographed. It's amazing what you can do with filters." He put the birchbark back in the box and handed Neil a photograph. "It's a very good map. Much better than the one Alexander drew from memory. It not only confirmed that we were working on the right island, but it led us straight to the right spot. I'd like to take you over and show you the exact site as soon as you're able to navigate."

Neil looked at the photograph of the map. There was a sense of unreality in all this. "So you've found the place? But why did the Indians have a map, if they didn't have a treasure to hide? What's so special about *this* place?"

"Every man's idea of treasure is different. I never did think that the mysterious Indian treasure was gold or jewels. The idea of hoarding valuables of that kind just doesn't fit the Indian philosophy. Their idea of treasure would be likely to be something much deeper. This bag now — it's a medicine bag, like the one you found in the MacAlpine cellar. From the piece of bone we've been able to date it. It's about four thousand years old. It's a terrific find."

"Four thousand years!" Neil was staggered. He reached out a finger and gently touched the bag. It was as dry as a mummy and covered with the same red dust that had been on the bag he had found in the cellar. "How come this didn't all rot away in the damp?"

"They were in sealed urns. This shard would have been part of one."

"But what does it *mean*?"

"Magic. Religion. Medicine. You can't really separate them. We know that medicine bags were in use when the white man came to America. But we had no idea they had been in use so long before."

"And you don't know what it means?"

"Not really. Perhaps medicine was the most potent force holding the Indian tribes together. As much a part of their life as the cult of the dead was to the Egyptians. You understand?"

Neil nodded. It was all very interesting, but he felt disappointed. "So this was the treasure?" He said flatly.

"Yes. Buried for safe keeping, perhaps, in some time

of danger. But that's not the whole of it, Neil. We think there's more. We're working on it right now and as soon as you're well enough you must come over and see for yourself. I must go now." He smiled, picked up the box and left.

Neil felt flat and tired and his leg ached abominably. His father chatted to him and he forced himself to answer. When he was at last alone he lay and looked at the ceiling and tried to work out his feelings.

"Oh, Mother, I feel such a fraud," he burst out as soon as she came into the room that evening. "I thought I was doing it all for Mrs. MacAlpine. But I wasn't at all. It was really the treasure I was excited about all the time!"

His mother smiled at him. "Oh, I doubt that, Neil. Of course you're disappointed. You could hardly go through all you went through looking for the treasure, without imagining the kind of treasure it was. People do that sort of thing all the time. Looking for jobs. Houses. Husbands and wives even. The secret is to forget about the imaginary pictures you've built up once you've found the real thing. Don't let your false image get in the way of your enjoyment of the real thing. You did find something very important, believe me. As for Mrs. MacAlpine, she's so excited! A reporter has been out to the house to get the whole story about

Alexander. They are going to put it in the weekend paper. It might even make the National Supplement."

"So then everyone will know the truth about old Alexander." Neil could feel the smile tugging at his face. "Oh, Mother, thank you. That's just great. It really was worth it after all."

CHAPTER TWELVE

It was almost a month before Neil was released from hospital in a walking cast, and another long week before he received the eagerly awaited invitation from Dr. Williams.

"I hope you weren't put off, waiting so long," the archaeologist explained, as he drove Neil across the temporary work bridge connecting the island to the mainland. "We found what we'd hoped for, and I wanted to get it all cleaned up before we showed you."

He parked the car and helped Neil out. "As you see, this island really is the shape of Alexander's sketch. What gave you the idea of hunting on that unpromising hunk of rock upstream?"

Neil explained how Jamie and he had seen the name

Treasure Island on the plan in the Project office. Dr. Williams laughed.

"Oh, that life should be so simple! I imagine that name is probably no more than fifty years old or so. Canadian place names have changed so much, as waves of different people passed through. And it's still all so new. Now in Arabia a place name like that might be a jolly good clue. But not here, I'm afraid. The ground's very rough over here. Can you manage?"

With his crutches and Dr. William's help Neil managed to limp from the car to the western tip of the island. The ground was mostly solid rock up here. The bulldozers could have uncovered nothing. But at the very tip of the island the working crew had rigged up a shelter of canvas, and here, in a deep niche in the rock, like a natural grave, lay, half-buried in reddish sand, a skeleton. It lay curled up on its side. The bones were coloured red and there was red in the sparse soil scattered around.

"Red ochre," Dr. Williams explained. "Obviously part of their ceremonial."

Half a dozen small clay pots, sealed and decorated with the same red ochre, stood in a semi-circle about the head of the skeleton. There were arrow heads heaped by the right hand, and lying among the ribs was an ornament of beaten iron.

"Meteoric iron." Dr. Williams pointed. "It would be a thing of great power, you see, having fallen from the sky. This must have been a very great chief. See how he lies alone at the extreme tip of the island. Gazing west. Facing upstream. We can only guess at the significance. But his presence here must have been handed down by word of mouth through the generations. Then eventually these people either died out or moved away, and a new people moved in. They would hear and pass on the distorted story of a treasure. A very great treasure."

Neil stood, leaning on his crutches, looking upstream. There was really nothing more to say. The sun shone gold on the river, bringing tears to his eyes.

Mrs. MacAlpine made their last evening into a farewell feast. "Thank you, boys, for all you've done. And not just for the doing, you ken, but for the kind and thoughtful hearts that made you want to do it. I can really hold my head up again at last."

The next day they stood with Mother and Father on the platform at Morrisburg waiting for the Toronto train. People who had seen their pictures in the weekend papers kept coming up to shake their hands and talk to them. Neil felt stupid shaking hands with all those strangers. This moment half way between home and school was an odd enough feeling at the best of times. He wished the train would hurry.

"Who are those boys everyone's fussing over?" He heard a querulous voice behind him.

"They're the kids that found the Indian graves. Staying over at MacAlpine's, you know."

"Her!" The voice was contemptuous. "You'd think she'd know better than to push herself into the limelight. After what her grandfather did and all."

Neil bit his lip and looked at his mother, his face flushed with anger. She put her arm round his shoulders.

"Shush. There's nothing you can do, Neil. Prejudice will always run one step ahead of truth, it seems. The best you can do is go on believing in the truth yourself and hunting for it, whatever."

"Come hell or high water, in fact, Mother." Their laughter was drowned in the whistle of the Toronto train.